Urban Creatures

Sarah Gray

Illustrations by Alodie Fielding

Published by:

Mercuria Press
www.mercuriapress.com
an imprint of
Chin Music Press
1501 Pike Place #329
Seattle, WA 98101-1542
www.chinmusicpress.com

First (1) edition
ISBN paperback: 978-1-63405-033-3

Design by Carla Girard & Ginny Wood
Cover and story illustrations © 2022 Alodie Fielding

Printed in Canada at Imprimerie Gauvin
Library of Congress Control Number: 2022935667

*For the
National Health Service
of the United Kingdom.*

*Thank you to all the staff at the NHS for
their care, skill and hard work: they are an
incredible team of professionals.*

URBAN CREATURES

Sarah Gray

Illustrations by Alodie Fielding

Mercuria Press

2022

Table of Contents

KILLING RACHEL

The music was loud. People laughed, mouthing the words of "Rolling in the Deep" at one another. A woman danced on the table, holding her drink high like a sacrificial goblet. It swayed with the music, the liquid threatening to leap from the glass onto the heads of spectators.

"Get this down your neck." Belinda, a work friend, pushed a shot into Rachel's hand. Rachel checked for the emergency exits. There were four. Her nearest was next to the bar. How could anyone get out of here in an emergency? Any hesitation from the security staff and it would be another Bradford disaster. Rachel could see the headlines: FIFTY-SIX DIE IN NIGHTCLUB INFERNO.

She sank backwards into the leather sofa; it consumed her, sucking her in. A drunken couple fell across her, kissing with wide mouths and visible tongues. Jimmy lifted his hand, placing it on the top of her head. Her ears flinched at each beat of the music. As it merged with the sounds of human exhilaration it deadened into silence. Sweat dripped down her back; she wanted to wipe it away as she breathed deeper and deeper, struggling for air. She felt dizzy, small sparkly dots leaping up and down before her eyes. Jimmy pulled her backwards, downwards. Gravity suckled her body, sapping its essence. She wanted to cry out, knowing the sound would only be absorbed into the darkness, cherished greedily by the void. The hand clamped about her skull, an even application of pressure wrapping itself around her brain, careful caresses that gently squeezed. No fixed point, freefalling, body limp, devoid of purpose. The hand tightened its hold, her eyes dimmed, the light-particles increased as her heart pounded ever more harshly, a hard thump violently clashing with an intense but deep pulse. The abyss devoured her. She gasped for any breath it permitted her to make: shallow, short, desperate. The light extinguished, the sound and silence crushed her. The couple were an indistinguishable outline, blending and fading to blackness as Rachel's body lost power. She tried to stand but fell to the floor. Crawling forward, she grasped a pair of legs.

"Help me. Please. Help me."

Rachel opened her eyes. The room was white; its brightness made it difficult to see any details. The bed was comfortable and warm. Confusion flooded her mind. What was she doing in bed, a bed she didn't know, in a place she didn't recognise? A club, she'd been in a club. Realisation dawned: this must be a hospital ward. She was relieved. At last she'd had an attack someone had taken seriously. Now she'd get a diagnosis. All those who doubted her would be sorry.

"A trick of the mind," that doctor at the Accident and Emergency had said. But temporarily losing her sight had led her to expect a brain tumour at the very least. Or even Mad Cow Disease, which would definitely be her mum's fault for feeding her all those cheap burgers as a kid. What a show she'd put on. Snivelling and blubbing like a baby, she'd made the nurse stay with her, holding her hand while she recounted every last detail of her health fears. "I can give you something to reduce your anxiety," the doctor had offered, poised to write a prescription. She didn't need drugs; she just needed to know what was wrong with her.

On leaving the hospital Rachel had marched straight into the nurse.

"Glad to see you're still alive. Take it easy," the nurse mocked. If only she could see Rachel now.

Her eyes began to adjust to the light. The room was beautifully decorated in Regency style. Being an interior designer, Rachel was used to seeing period interpretations, but this was perfect. It was no NHS room. This must be an exclusive private establishment to be decorated in such a grand manner.

However, it was a strange hospital that had pictures of Death decorating its walls. All four images showed personifications of Death. The first was of a delicate young boy. Underneath it read: *Hellenic, Thanatos*. The next, *Hindu, King Yama or King of Karmic Justice*, depicted a figure riding a black buffalo and carrying a rope lasso. A feminine skeletal form wearing a crown and surrounded by flowers was called *La Santa Muerte* or *Saint Death*.

Finally, the figure of *The Grim Reaper* stared down at her. Death was carrying a large scythe and clothed in a black cloak and hood. Rachel wondered how many variations there could be: as many as there were belief systems, possibly.

She heard the door handle slowly being turned and stared at the door. It suddenly flung open, banged against the wall and deflected back into its frame, smacking the person on the threshold. For a flash, Rachel saw a figure all in black and heard a grunt of pain. Another moment passed. The door now gently began to open. Emerging from behind it was a young man. Slim and tall, his skin so pale it was touched with blue, his brow knotted above black eyes, he edged forward with small steps, stopping and pulling at his robe as if it were snagged on a branch. He held out his right hand. Rachel stared, looking from his right hand to his left: the left was much larger. Jimmy flushed red, withdrew it, and placed his enlarged hand behind his back.

"I'm afraid you're dead." He mumbled it, refusing to meet her eyes.

"Dead?"

"Yeah, dead." He nodded.

"Really? Dead?" Rachel looked at her hands, and down at her body. "I don't feel dead. You sure?" She was grabbing parts of her body.

"Well, in-limbo dead." It sounded like an apology.

"Limbo dead?" Rachel screwed up her nose.

"I'm afraid there's been a terrible mistake." He looked to the floor and again blushed.

"Tea?" Jimmy asked as he hovered the teapot above the delicate china cup and saucer set in front of her.

"Erm, yes please." Rachel watched as the liquid filled her cup. She looked up at Jimmy and watched his face, serious as he concentrated on his task.

"Milk? Sugar?" he enquired.

"No, sweet enough. So what was it in the end?" She stared at him, raising her eyebrows.

"In the end?" Jimmy had no idea what she meant. He was also unused to being glared at by an attractive young woman. How was he expected to think under such circumstances? She didn't wait for his reply.

"Brain tumour? Thrombosis? No, no, no, let me guess, it must have been a stroke." He frowned and put down the teapot.

"I told you it was a mis ..." He stopped.

"A 'mis'? A 'mis' what?" She was impatient.

"A mysterious type of stroke, that was it." He nodded. "Yes, that was definitely it."

"I knew it!" Almost shouting, she knocked the table as she stood up. Tea splashed into the saucer. "I knew there was something wrong. I bet they're all sorry now." Her glee was alarming to Jimmy. He'd never seen someone so happy to be dead.

"'They'? Who are 'they'?" He was confused.

"Family, friends, doctors. You know, anyone who didn't believe me." She'd shown them they were all wrong by up and dying on them. They'd be sorry now! And at last, maintaining her exhausting pretence of "successful young woman in control of her life" was over. She breathed a sigh of relief.

"Oh, I see. Yes, well, sorry, but not in the way you mean, I guess." Her zeal overwhelmed him.

"And you're 'The Caretaker' and you look after those who come to live in limbo?"

"Erm, yes, sorry, you'll have to put up with me for the time being." His laugh was nervous, and he shrugged his shoulders, raising his eyebrows as he spoke.

"And I'm in limbo because it hasn't been decided by the powers that be, whoever they are, what's going to happen to me?"

"Yes, right again." Coughing slightly, he concentrated on replacing his cup into its saucer.

"How come I'm in limbo? Where will I go? How long will it take?" Her familiar vertigo rose. Death was beginning to make less sense than life.

Her knowledge of afterlife options was limited. She was not religious and didn't believe in God, or rather not the Christian god presented to her as a child. School assembly, when they'd all mumbled the Lord's Prayer and sang a handful of hymns, was the nearest she'd come to any kind of worship. Fluffy clouds with cherubs lounging around, playing miniature harps was the limit of her imagination. And then she considered the alternative. Naked people tied to stakes, fire licking up their bodies, their screams piercing and desperate. She shuddered.

"Don't worry, it will be okay." He tried to smile.

"That's not really an answer, is it?" Confusion and uncertainty seemed to permeate both sides of the divide.

"Well, no, yes, but…"

This girl was going to be troublesome. She had been such a diligent anxiety sufferer for him, one of his better clients really; he'd had no idea she'd be so assertive. Death's Scythe hadn't worked how he'd imagined, and now he was stuck with her until he could work out how to finish the job he'd started, without Death finding out his intention to keep killing. Or discovering Rachel before he entirely killed her. How he was going to keep her quiet, hiding her in Death's house, he wasn't yet sure.

Purveyor of panic attacks, red mists and black dogs. Jimmy sighed and replaced his business card into his wallet.

"A lot of good it does me. It's all right for you. People look up to you: they respect and fear you. But me, they think they've a physical ailment, trying to give their miseries a tangible cause. All my good work wasted." Jimmy stared into his china teacup, his shoulders hunched forward causing his black robe to fall down about the tops of his arms. He sat in one of two wing back chairs that were positioned in front of the iron fireplace. Death's study was elegant, if modelled on a Sherlock Holmes Victoriana. Book shelves were lined with leather-bound editions and the walls adorned with red-wine flock paper.

Death sat next to Jimmy, perched on the arm of the chair. His slender fingers curled around his shoulders. "Look Jimmy, you do a really important job, and you're good at it. You remind people of their fallibility, that life is at times ... let's say ... difficult, and pain is inevitable. Because of the misery you bring, people understand happiness when it comes to them. Because of your pain, they value the goodness in life. There cannot be one without the other. You are necessary for humanity to be human."

"That's not true and you know it. I'm just something to be swept under the carpet. No one brags about the amazing panic attacks or the feelings of utter hopelessness they just experienced. It's just not the done thing."

Death picked up his cup and sat in the chair opposite to Jimmy. "Wonderful blend of tea by the way. What about the suicides? There's something to think about."

"No, it's not. Where's the nobility in that? It's not quite the same as dying after a long, brave fight with cancer. That has romance. I'm just not useful, glamorous or imposing. I'm an embarrassment."

"That's not true, Jimmy. Everyone here has a crucial role and you really are doing a fantastic job. There are people living with terrible depressions across the globe and all thanks to you. Why can't you just be yourself? You'll make yourself ill trying to be something you're not, and, if the robe fits ..." Death glanced at his brother's sagging garment and continued, "Your sisters are happy with their jobs."

"That might be something to do with them being spirits of violent death. Battle, accident, and murder are so much juicier than suicide."

"Juicy, yes, ah, I see. Anyway, this is what you were created to do. Give it time, you may come to enjoy it again. If not, I'll put a word in for you, see if we can't get your duties expanded a little."

"Really? Would you? I'd be so grateful, Jules. And I'd love a scythe like yours." Jimmy pretended to cut through the air with his imaginary scythe.

"We've been through this. The Scythe of Death is a unique tool. What's wrong with your enlarged hand, anyway? Jolly dandy, I've always thought, and at least you don't have the burden of carrying a scythe around. Now, I want to hear no more about this until you've given it your best effort. Off you go."

As the door closed on Jimmy, Jules sighed in frustration. He wondered how long it would take for Jimmy to confess his "mistake".

Limbo consisted of two rooms. When she'd imagined being dead she certainly didn't foresee being confined to a bedroom and living room and treated like a pampered prisoner. Jimmy jumped at every noise and kept the doors locked. Standing at the large French windows, she stared out into the garden. The garden was serene and reminded her of those she'd seen on visits to English stately homes. Roses of pink, yellow and crimson red framed the doorway, and beyond a small patio were rows of intricately crafted topiary. In the distance she could see the top of a large domed glasshouse. Rachel tried the door handles. Locked. But then, she knew that already.

"Er, herm, Rachel, it's your turn." Jimmy was sitting at the table. In front of him was a Scrabble board. He was smiling.

"I just put down 'DEAD'. It was worth six points. Not

too bad, I think you'll admit." He was nodding, pleased with himself. Rachel looked at the board.

"I guess it's okay, but if you had laid it the other way you could have got the triple word score." Jimmy stopped smiling. His eyes darted from one part of the board to the other.

"Where?" He continued searching as Rachel picked up her counters and covered a triple word score.

"You just don't think it through, Jimmy. Strategy isn't your strong point and your poker face is terrible." Rachel affected the smug head tilt of a winner.

"See, DEATH." Mumbling numbers, she calculated her score. "Twenty-seven points. There you go, that's how to play the game." She laughed. This was the first time she'd played board games and loved it. When alive she'd never made time for games. If it wasn't about her career then she hadn't bothered, not being able to see the point. Games were fun. But Jimmy lashed out, pushing the board away from him. Counters slid across the smooth surface and came to rest, creating yet to be discovered words.

"How's that for strategy?" He folded his arms and turned his head away.

"You'll never win if you don't have a plan."

He snorted. "Well, maybe that's your problem: you're too cold and calculating."

"What do you mean by that?" Rachel was surprised.

"With all your plans and schemes, there's no room to enjoy yourself."

"What?! You're 'The Caretaker' and you're supposed to look after me, but all we've done is play Scrabble and you ALWAYS get upset 'cause I ALWAYS win. And I still have no idea what I'm doing in limbo and what's going to happen to me. Under the circumstances, I think I'm pretty relaxed."

"What did you expect? It *is* limbo."

"I didn't expect it to be like an eternal Christmas afternoon playing Scrabble with my bad loser of a little brother." They were both standing up, facing each other.

"You're just like my brother—I try really hard and you don't appreciate me." Jimmy grabbed a handful of tiles and threw them into the box where they bounced in all directions. "I don't know why I bother." He reached forward and scraped the escapee letters towards himself. The stress of keeping Rachel a secret and maintaining his regular duties was beginning to play havoc with his nerves.

Rachel smiled. "Now you sound like my mother."

"At least you have a mother." Jimmy kept his gaze fixed on a tile marked with the letter S, tears welling in his eyes.

Rachel started to laugh. "Oh Jimmy, I'm sorry." She touched him on the hand. He pulled it away slowly, leaving her finger resting on the S.

"Okay. Apology accepted." He looked at her from lowered lids. Rachel bounded up to him.

"Why don't we go out? I think we need it. We're going to go crazy locked up in here. And it's only been four days."

"I don't think so." He avoided her eager stare.

"Oh Jimmy, why not?" He couldn't risk Jules seeing them. "Please, please, please. I'll teach you how to beat me at chess and Scrabble. Strategy will be your middle name." She looked up at him with pleading eyes.

"Oh alright, but you must do as I say, and get out of sight if need be. Understand?"

The sky was clear and blue. It was enormous and stretched for eternity. To Rachel, it was like the Sunday afternoon skies when she had been a child, and the sun was yellow and hot and kept her warm even without a cardigan. Gravel crunched under her feet and she wanted to ask Jimmy if they could have an ice cream. It would complete her picture of a perfect summer's afternoon: a memory formed before her father had gone away. Plants climbed the garden walls, creating protective layers from the out-side world—whatever the world outside of limbo might be. Green surrounded them, with dots of colour dripping from each stem or branch. It was sumptuous. She felt calm with a peace that she rarely knew. Limbo was so bland that it rendered any of her fears unfounded, and her quiet routine of games and chats was eroding her sharp edges. If this was death, then nothing else bad could happen to her. She no longer needed to prove herself to anyone. Jimmy towered over her, and it was as if she was walking next to nobody with his head so far above hers. Rachel watched him for a moment. He could have been made from a "how to build the ideal human kit"—except that something in the assembly had gone awry. If he hadn't been so extreme in opposites, he would be beautiful. But his eyes were a little too dark and his cheeks a little too sharp. His too pale skin accentuated his too chiselled face. And he shuffled, round-shouldered, as if he knew he was the remaindered version of a man, a blurred photocopy of the template. He kept his enlarged hand behind his back and pointed with the other.

"That's the *Gallica* or Rose of Provins."

Hanging from the wall were a huddle of deep-pink roses whose fine petals layered and curled into one another.

"Very pretty." Leaning in, she tried to smell them but stumbled forward. He caught hold of her arm with his enlarged hand.

"It's usually me that falls." He giggled, embarrassed as he set her on her feet, and withdrew his hand, placing it behind his back. He continued.

"They're often called The Apothecary's Rose, *R. gallica officinalis*, and were grown in the Middle Ages in monastic herbaria for their alleged medicinal properties. They eventually became famous in English history as the Red Rose of Lancaster." His laugh was nervous. "Or so I've heard." He blushed.

"Wow, I'm impressed. I don't know anything about flowers and trees. Interiors are more my area." Rachel thought of her flat. It was immaculate, beautiful. She'd designed it herself with exacting care. Months of agonising debate, years of intense mental visualisation. Colour schemes, fabrics, flooring. All designed to balance light and mood to reflect her unique character and image.

"You're like my brother. He loves to decorate, he's always at it. That's why the house is immaculate. I prefer nature. It's just so ..." Unable to think of the word, he frowned and fell silent for a moment. Then repeated, "It's just so."

"'Just so'? Don't you mean 'just is'?" Rachel screwed up her nose.

"No, I don't. For example, there are over a hundred types of roses and thousands of cultivars. And they're all perfect. They have a place and a function that fits with the rest of nature. It just works."

"But the advantage with decorating is creating perfection yourself. I'm in total control when I design a room: I decide on everything and make it happen. Nothing is overlooked and that's all down to me."

"That's a very limited idea of perfection."

Rachel scrutinised him. This was a very different Jimmy than the one who threw Scrabble pieces around the room.

"I need to show you something." He walked to the exit and stuck his head out, looking both ways before leading her through the doorway. Bobbing her head down to avoid the roses that hung from the frame, she followed him. In front was the entrance to a huge glasshouse. It stood at least 200 feet high, and reminded her of the top part of the club from a suit of cards. An ornate cast iron spire reached into the sky, as if to pop clouds. Hundreds, maybe even thousands of these glasshouses lined the path, shrinking as they receded into the distance.

"Bloody hell." Rachel was flabbergasted. She'd only ever seen one glasshouse at a time and it was impressive enough on its own. Jimmy nodded, smiling.

"Why on earth—or in limbo—are there so many?"

"Where else do you think all the plant life that has ever existed is kept?" Jimmy brimmed with satisfaction.

"To be fair, Jimmy, I've never thought about it before. I just assumed they'd be on earth and gone forever when, you know, they died."

"It's amazing, isn't it?" He gestured with arms wide. "You can find anything you want, from any point in history."

"But how? There's so many of them." Bright beams reflected on the glass. Shielding her eyes from the glare, she stared up the path towards the receding buildings.

Jimmy beamed with pride again. "The Gardener is very good with databases, as well as plants. This is one of my faves." He beckoned her along as he marched down the path. Rachel followed, half running behind him, curious at what Jimmy was so excited to share with her.

"How much longer?" Rachel whined, stopping to remove a stone from her shoe.

"You were nagging to get outside, now you're moaning about being out."

"My feet hurt in these shoes. I just don't have the right footwear for this."

"Here we are." Jimmy stopped in front of a glasshouse and pointed to a sign. Rachel read it aloud.

"Fungi, English, Extinct 1820–2015." Placing his hands on the brass handles, Jimmy pushed open the doors.

Musty with the richness of moist earth, the smell was overwhelming. Rachel stood in the middle of a British woodland. Trees reached up to the roof, deep-green ferns spread across the ground, and fungi of all types bred between mosses. The light was dim and the air damp. They were completely insulated. Misshapen growths twisted from tree trunks, and toadstools that could have been conjured by fairies huddled together around her feet. She laughed.

"It's like pixieland." Nature had created a messy and gnarled form of perfection. Rachel thought it beautiful.

Jimmy bent down and pulled back some fern leaves. Beneath was a cluster of bright-purple domes, small white blotches spread over their curves.

"These are *Cortinarius cumatilis*. They became extinct in 1868." Rachel bent down beside him.

"They're incredible." She smiled at Jimmy.

"Yes, they are, and just think, you'd never have seen them if you hadn't come here." He stood up and put his hands on his hips. "Over seventy varieties of fungi have become extinct in the UK during the last 200 years."

"How do you know all of this? It's impressive, Jimmy. You're rubbish at Scrabble, but you're magic at this stuff." Jimmy glowed red and grinned.

"The Gardener is a friend of mine, and she lets me help out a bit. I find it relaxing." Rachel watched him as he wandered further into the wood.

"It's more than that, Jimmy." She followed him, tottering amongst the fungi, wobbling as she placed one foot in front of the other. He shouted without looking back.

"Watch out for the large pink one on your left. *Hygrophorus russula* or Pinkmottle Woodwax, extinct 1903. She's quite a beauty."

As she followed Jimmy further into the woods, she noticed the walls of the glasshouse had ceased to contain them, and they seamlessly merged and became a large wood. Instead of fungi, small blue flowers were sprouting from the ground. Blue overtook green until the entire floor of the wood was smothered in small violet-blue bells.

"Everything is always okay in the woods." Jimmy was staring down at the flowers.

"Yes, it is," she said. They stood in silence for a moment. Speaking with Jimmy was easy; she felt no need to impress him or fear of saying the wrong thing.

"So why doesn't your brother appreciate you when you're part of all this?"

Jimmy turned away from her and then shrugged.

"All this isn't my job and all Jules is interested in is duty." He wouldn't face her.

"He doesn't see what you're capable of, thinks you're young and idiotic, and your feelings count for nothing?" Her mum didn't even make an attempt at concealing this was how she felt about Rachel. Nipping to Ikea and throwing a few matching cushions on the sofa was her mother's idea of interior design. Art college was an expensive indulgence, according to her. She never realised how hard Rachel had worked at college and to get her first break. The harder Rachel worked, the less it counted.

Jimmy's lips tugged upwards at her sarcasm.

"Yes, I suppose. Don't get me wrong, I love him and all that. He looks after me, sort of, and I respect what he does … he's awfully efficient." Jimmy stopped.

"But?" Rachel walked towards him, trying to get a better look at his expression.

"But, he doesn't understand my job. At all. It's okay for him, he's the big cheese around here and in the Living World, no one has any choice but to obey him, but nobody respects what I do. It's just not cool." He stooped down and plucked a flower from the top of its stem. A love god, or god of war, anything would be better than being the god of petty miseries.

"They're endangered, you know." Rachel smiled. Jimmy looked into the palm of his hand, bewildered.

"Oh, yes. Of course, silly me." He frowned.

"They're not here." Rachel grinned at him.

"It was a joke, I see, yes." They smiled at one another.

"So you're sad because you're not cool?" Rachel asked. Jimmy stared at her.

"Yes, no, of course not. I'd like more responsibility but he never listens. I never seem to do enough to impress him; I only ever disappoint him." Jimmy sighed.

"Well, I think you're doing a good job of looking after me. I'd never have seen all this—" Rachel spun around and stopped directly in front of Jimmy, "—if you hadn't shown it to me." Jimmy glowed with pleasure and then shrugged and shook his head and turned away.

"But it's not …" He stumbled into silence again, he couldn't tell her what he really did.

"Is that why you're embarrassed of your hand? Being less than perfect isn't cool?" Looking at the tiny crushed flower in his palm, he ignored her.

"This is *Hyacinthoides non-scripta*. It was named after Hyacinth, lover of the god Apollo. As Hyacinth lay dying, this flower sprang from his blood. Apollo marked the petals with his tears of grief and the marks spelled the word, 'alas.'"

"That's so sad." She listened to the wood pigeon cooing its rhythmic song. "You know, Jimmy, I think being good at board games is over-rated."

Jimmy waited for a moment and listened. He couldn't hear anything. Jules should be having his nap at this time. Satisfied he wouldn't be interrupted, he gently lifted the brass catch and pulled the cabinet door open. The Scythe was nestled in its black velvet cradle. It was an awe-inspiring object. He'd thought through all the alternatives. Jimmy considered asking his sisters, but they were mean and would probably tell Jules. They told him everything. And he knew he had to go through with the job he'd started. Taking Rachel back home would be an anti-climax. And she did seem pleased to be dead.

Grabbing the Scythe, he turned it in the air, dropped it to ground level and began to mow from left to right. It floated, perfectly balanced. Jimmy spun around, holding the Scythe in front of him. He laughed. The feeling was amazing. He fantasised about cutting hundreds of people down in a single action. He continued his fanciful cull, swishing the tool back and forth. He'd be a real god. A god that other gods bowed down to. He'd be awe-inspiring and not some pathetic loser.

Again, he ran the Scythe back and forth in the air. He'd be good at this, killing people. Maybe not as good as Jules, at least not at the beginning, but he'd soon perfect his technique and develop his own unique style. He could absolutely do this. He imagined rows of people in front of him and mowing them down. He imagined cutting Rachel down.

He suddenly felt sick. Jimmy let the Scythe drop to the ground, halting his imaginary harvest. Dizzy and nauseous he pressed his hand against his stomach, confused. Gods don't get food poisoning. They don't get flu or pick up parasites. Listlessly, he swung the Scythe through the air again. Rachel. She had to die. He had to kill her. Had to. And only the Scythe could do it.

He didn't actually want Rachel to leave. She was much better at Scrabble, which did annoy him, but he liked having her around. He enjoyed being responsible for her.

He couldn't kill her.

Rachel ran her hand along the row of DVDs; there were hundreds of them. All comedies: Laurel and Hardy, The Three Stooges, Bing Crosby and Bob Hope's *On the Road* collection. She closed her eyes and plucked one from the shelf.

"*Mr. Bean's Holiday.*" She turned it over in her hand. "Do you actually like this stuff? I hate slapstick. It's so childish."

"It's actually quite sophisticated, I think you'll find. And requires a lot of skill to perform." Plucking the film from her hand, he put it back on the shelf.

"Really? Argh. All that faffing around. He stands up and knocks the other one down, who then in turn drops everything he's holding, which ruins all the work they've done. It's infuriating—can't they get anything right?"

"Precisely. Who can fall over at just the right moment to set a chain of chaos into action? Anyway, why should there be conditions on what makes you laugh? If it's funny, you laugh. I'll show you." Jimmy ran his finger along the shelf and pulled out *Duck Soup*. "Unless you're resisting, and that's a different thing."

"No, really, do we have to?" Rachel slumped down on the far end of the sofa and laid her head back, rolling it around like a small child avoiding the request to complete an unwelcome task.

"I promise you'll be laughing by the end. It's a classic."

"Usually that means tedious and outdated. And why the DVDs? It's so old school."

"I like to collect physical objects." He placed the disc into the machine. "There's no harm in watching, is there? Give it a go, you might even enjoy it."

"Okay … I guess so. It might be nice not to have to think about anything."

"How gracious of you." He pressed play on the remote control and sat at the opposite end of the sofa as the music began.

Rachel was watching Jimmy laugh. It was always a loud outburst followed by silence, accompanied by him holding onto his stomach as if he had appendicitis, his entire body shaking as it bobbed up and down. Tears rolled down his cheeks and dripped onto his robe. This had been going on for the past forty-five minutes.

"How can anything be that funny?" Incredulous at the mess in front of her, Rachel stared. He made an attempt to control himself, breathing in hard, then panting noiselessly fast. Jimmy burst out laughing again and pointed at her, unable to form any words. He flapped his hands up and down as if it would steady him. Unable to help herself, her face cracked into a grin. Jimmy pointed at her again. She broke into laughter. Surprised, she attempted to compose herself.

"See! You're laughing," he accused her.

"At you, not the film," she corrected.

"It doesn't matter, you're still laughing. So it is the film. It made me laugh and that made you laugh."

"That's cheating." At the same moment they both burst into laugher again but a loud knock interrupted. Jimmy stopped immediately.

"We never get visitors …"

"Shush," Jimmy cut her off. He took long strides across the floor and stood behind the door.

"Who is it?" he shouted at the closed door.

"Cousin, your brother requires your attention. Immediately." The voice was female, unusually deep and soporific.

"Alright, I'll be along in a minute."

"He says I must return with you," the voice insisted.

"Does he? Well …"

"His mood is splenetic, James. May I enter?" Jimmy shoved his shoulder into the door as it started to open. It slammed shut.

"Obviously not," the voice continued.

"I'll come, just give me a second. I've been exercising." Rachel laughed and Jimmy glared at her.

"Do not jest. He is bellicose." The voice was stern.

"Okay, I'm coming." Jimmy stood up straight, smoothed his robe with both of his hands, turned to face the door, took a deep breath, and left the room.

Rachel had been shocked at the change in Jimmy. He'd gone from laughing to the point of asphyxiation to looking like the life was being drained from him. She was amazed he could get any paler. His brother must be a tyrant if he had that effect on him. When he'd told her about his brother, she'd underestimated how he felt. Now Rachel wasn't surprised that Jimmy was so nervous. And it didn't seem fair that his brother held him back so much. She'd only known him a few weeks but he was definitely more complex than she'd first thought. Families can be so difficult. Her mother had married within a year of her dad leaving, and although her stepdad was okay, it had been hard to adjust to life under a new regime. His authority was unwanted and she resented having her mother's attention taken away from her. Security was something she could no longer take for granted. Within a year her brother, Danny, had been born. The happy nuclear family complete with a gurgling junior made her feel like the cuckoo in her own nest. The result was she told them nothing and was determined to prove she could be a success without them. When, in her first year of university, she'd fallen pregnant she told no one and silently dealt with the problem alone. Surface infallibility was her protection. But it was such hard work to face everything alone. Rachel decided she'd find a way to help Jimmy. She would encourage him to confront his brother and get his job changed.

"You love her? Honest to goodness, Jimmy, this situation goes from bad to worse." Jules had become impatient at waiting for Jimmy's confession, but he'd never expected a declaration of love. He admitted to himself he couldn't understand Jimmy at all.

"I want her to stay here with us. For good." Jimmy held his hands clasped together in front of him, anticipating disaster. He kept his gaze fixed on Jules's stationery; his pens were lined up on his desk in straight rows: everything he did was perfect. Death drew in a long breath. He'd been working on an official complaint from Odin that Minerva had interfered with his plans for war in the Middle East. She had counter claimed that he was "over zealous" and they could all do with a break. As if that wasn't enough, Dionysus was boring the Dryads with his tedious drunken stories. They complained he was no longer good company. Jesus had been hanging about his office too. He was a nice chap but Death wished he'd get to the point more directly: his stories were not the most efficient way of getting things done. Gods and their petty problems had been a constant burden to him. And now Jimmy. Again. Jules stared at him from the far side of his desk, affecting peaceful calm.

"Not only did you take the Scythe and attempted, poorly, I might add, to kill a human, but now this. How you thought I'd never notice is a mystery. I've allowed you enough rope and it's time to sort it out. And after all I said to you." Standing up, Death wasn't sure if he should shake Jimmy or not.

"I'm sorry. Sorry, sorry. Are you angry?" Jimmy kept his eyes lowered, looking at the ground.

"Not angry, just disappointed." Death contained his frustration, holding it back with the strength of his clenched jaw. Jimmy doubted he was "just disappointed".

"Does she love you?" Jules asked with a hint of derision.

"It's complicated."

"So what exactly is your plan? Hold her captive here until she starts asking uncomfortable questions?" Filling his pipe, the abundant tobacco spilled onto his tweed trousers. Jules brushed it from his trousers with the tips of his slender fingers. Similar to his immaculate house, he was impeccably attired. He only wore his robes when on duty and to keep up appearances. In looks, the brothers resembled one another, although Jules was confident, with the well-assembled air of a World War Two RAF hero.

"She never stops asking uncomfortable questions. I just thought she, well, she might learn to love me." Jimmy flopped into the chair opposite Jules.

"Learn to love you? You're holding her hostage." Jules struggled to contain his disbelief. "You've got to sort this out. She must be returned to the human world immediately, and don't tell her anything about your 'mistake' or where she is. If you haven't already. Just get rid of her. There will be consequences for this, and you've got to show me you're responsible. This is your last chance."

"No. I want Rachel. I knew you wouldn't understand—you've never been in love. You're prejudiced against her because she's human, and all that death has twisted your mind. You can't tell me what to do. I won't let you! She's staying with me."

"I will take her without argument if you don't return her to the human world *now*."

Death watched as his younger brother tripped on the hem of his robe, stumbled sideways, and regained his composure before storming off, slamming the door behind him. Death lit his pipe and inhaled. He had been patient, but he couldn't let Jimmy continue like this. Jimmy didn't understand the danger he was in. It was true, Death did have the power of life and death, but there was only so much he could do. It was his job to maintain the balance of things; his hands were tied. Jimmy never seemed to understand that. It was such a shame; Jimmy had such potential. And he was his own flesh and blood after all. But the laws were the laws; there was no negotiation over them. Being sent to earth to become a mortal, his life reduced to a flash in the pan—it just wasn't fitting for Death's brother. Death would become a laughingstock. He would give Jimmy one last chance to do the right thing and then he would have to act on his words.

Rachel was lying on her bed trying to think of ways to help Jimmy stand up to his brother. It was difficult without really knowing what he was like. She wondered if Jimmy would introduce her. There was a quiet knock on the door.

"Is that you, Jimmy?" She got up and opened the door.

"Can I come in?" His eyes pleaded.

"Of course. You've been ages. Is your brother hassling you again?" Jimmy shrugged and turned away from her.

"You've got to stand up to him. Demand he gives you what you want."

"You really don't know my brother, it's not that easy."

"Maybe I could meet him, get a better idea of what makes him tick?"

"No, no, Rachel, that's really not a good idea at all.

Anyway, it's time to move on. Your fate has been decided."

"Oh." Rachel sat back on the bed and started flicking through the pages of a book.

"What does 'oh' mean? I thought you'd be pleased." He sat on the bed beside her.

"I am, but I'm starting to like it here." She kept her face turned away from him and continued plucking at the book.

"You do?" He grinned. "It's just, there are no other humans, only you. I thought you'd start to think it's strange that you're dead and there are no other dead people around." She lay back on the bed and put her arms behind her head.

"I don't mind, really." She rolled onto her side and propped up her head. It was true, she didn't mind. More than that, she was enjoying being freed from her innate talent of knocking the fun out of everything.

"Oh." He swallowed hard. "I'm so sorry. You have to move on, and I'm taking you."

"You're taking me? Okay, yes, at least that's something." She trailed off. He smiled and stood up to face her. "Where are we going?"

"To post-limbo. It's a training school for the afterlife. It will take us a couple of days to get there."

Instead of glorious sunshine, the moon shone bright and low, making the rose garden seem sinister and misshapen. It was odd that Jimmy had insisted they leave at night and bring very little with them but she didn't ask him any questions. He was so stressed about the journey it didn't seem fair to add to his worry. However, when he announced they'd be going on foot, she'd wondered how far they'd actually get. After having some time to think about it, "post-limbo" sounded a little odd too. But bringing it up at that moment would be awkward, Rachel decided. Repeating his earlier ritual, Jimmy stuck his head out of the doorway before venturing onto the pathway. The glasshouses loomed over them, dominating the skyline. Rachel felt they were watching the two of them, ushering them along, keeping them to the pathway. Above them the ink black sky was pricked with silver pinholes. Rachel wanted to stop and indulge in the uniqueness of each constellation. Formations revealed only by the dark. But Jimmy was hustling her on, habitually looking behind him, as if he expected to be followed.

Rachel was tired. They'd been walking for a long time and Jimmy had barely said a word. Reaching a break in the glasshouses, they turned a corner and an allotment lay ahead. It was as regimented as the glasshouses, but instead there were hundreds of rows of vegetables. Vines hung from canes built into structures to support their growth. Every plant was heavy with pods or beans, bushy leaves sprouting from the ground. It was luscious.

At the far end of the garden was a row of brick sheds. Small white-framed windows spotted the walls at regular intervals. As they approached, Jimmy reached up and took a key down from the top of the doorframe. He opened the door, bobbing down to enter. Inside was a miniature living room. Everything was slightly too small for an average-sized man so Jimmy looked enormous. In the centre of the room was a round wooden table with two chairs on either side. Behind it was a Welsh dresser and, next to that, a deep china sink. A single tap hovered above it. Behind the door was a narrow bed dressed with rough blankets. Jimmy put his bag down and picked up the kettle. He filled it with water.

"Cup of tea?" He lit a small gas stove and placed the kettle on it.

"Yes, please, I'm parched." Rachel flopped down at the table, her head collapsing onto her arms.

"Jimmy, what are we doing here?" He kept his back to her.

"Resting for the night."

She answered, unable to lift her head from fatigue. "Okay, but it all feels, well, a bit strange. It feels like we're running away."

Jimmy forced a laugh and turned around. "Of course not. Don't be silly."

"This place could be a secret hideout."

He sat down opposite her. The tops of his knees poked up over the table's surface.

"It's fine, Rachel. Enough." His voice was raised.

She'd never seen Jimmy angry before and she didn't like it.

Jimmy is walking along the street and everyone else is walking in the opposite direction. The pavement gets busier and people keep knocking into him. He starts to panic because he doesn't recognise anything or anyone, and the people look angry and mean and the jostling turns into pushing. A murmur permeates the crowds of people as they begin to whisper, "You can't run away, you can't escape." The whisper gets louder and louder until Jimmy shouts.

"Maude, get out of my head!"

Jimmy sat bolt up right and saw his cousin standing in front of his chair. "Why can't you just speak to me instead? The dream thing is too intimate."

Rachel stirred in the small camp bed. Jimmy held his breath, but Rachel turned over and continued to sleep.

"Apologies and do not worry, cousin. I have given her a very pleasing dream. She will not wake. I needed to find you urgently and this is by far the speediest method." Her deep voice rumbled through the cottage.

"Are you sure about the dream? Let's go outside." Jimmy ushered Maude from the cottage and led her to the back of the garden.

"My quest is to, if possible, dissuade you from your foolhardy mission. You cannot outwit Death, and he is furious. You know this well, as do I. He will send you to live amongst the mortals. James, you will die as a mortal. Is this what you want?" Jimmy stared at the ground, refusing to look at her. He didn't want to be mortal. A human's life was short and dull. Jimmy wanted to be a more impressive god with exciting powers. "I can see why Jules grows impatient with you. Do you want to give up your duties and forsake your family? There is no guarantee you will even know Rachel in the mortal world, and you will have given up everything for nothing in return. Where do you think you are even trying to go that Death will not follow?"

James kept his eye to the ground and mumbled, "To the love gods."

Maude frowned and lifted Jimmy's head up by his chin. "I cannot discern your words."

"TO THE LOVE GODS!" He folded his arms.

"Why you persist in acting like a human, I do not know. What help can they be to you?"

"Of course I don't want to be mortal, what's the point in that, as you say? But the love gods might know somewhere we can go to be together without HIM interfering."

"You are living in a world of dreams, James. You vex him at every turn." Jimmy smiled.

"A world of dreams. That's it, Maude! Maybe you could help us?"

"Do not even dare to think of it. You are my kin, James, and I love you, but even if I could sustain a dream that could be a home for you both, I would not dare to cross Death in such a way."

"You're here now, unless you're just his stooge, spying on us to tell him all about it."

"Oh James, I do not need to 'spy' as you say. I am attempting to help you keep your place amongst us, but I can see you need to learn your own lesson." Jimmy's shoulders slumped and his gown slipped around the top of his arm.

"Just keep him distracted until I can find out if there's a chance for us. I know he'll realise soon enough I haven't returned her yet, but help me. Please, Maude, please."

"I will try, but be swift in your task and promise me

that if the love gods tell you that there is nothing that can legally be done, you will give up this pursuit." Jimmy grabbed Maude and hugged her tight.

Maude continued as she struggled free. "If you are in need of me, James, you know how I can be contacted. Sleep well."

———⊸◦⊸———

It had put Jimmy in a good mood that Maude had helped him. Being a bit of a swot and devoted to Jules, she could have gone either way. He'd never have such reservations about help from Hegemone or, as he'd told Rachel, "The Gardener." They'd been friends for years and both shared a love of growing things. Jimmy was pottering around the room when Rachel opened her eyes. He took some plates down from the Welsh dresser and placed them with care on the table. In the centre was a basket piled with fresh bread rolls, and next to it a huge glass bowl overflowing with sumptuous summer fruits. Jimmy stood back and stared at the table arrangement as if admiring a work of art.

"Where did the food come from?"

Jimmy started as Rachel spoke. She laughed as Jimmy clutched at his chest. "You scared the life out of me. No need to laugh."

"Sorry, but your expression was a picture." Still laughing as she stood up, she reached over and plucked a fat cherry from the bowl. Struggling, he managed to rearrange his robe.

"Delicious cherries. And the bread smells amazing."

Rachel grabbed a handful of fruit.

"The Gardener brought us the food. She's agreed to ..." He stopped. "Help" might suggest something was wrong.

"She? I thought The Gardener would be a man, with a big beard." Rachel indicated a beard by rubbing her chin.

"Sexist." Jimmy pretended to pull on it.

"She's agreed to what?"

"Nothing, just gave us some provisions. For the journey."

"We did leave in a bit of a hurry, under the cloak of night."

"I just wanted to get a head ... a good start."

"On foot?" Rachel pointed to her thin leather ballet pumps. Jimmy grinned at her.

"Look outside."

Rachel moved to the door and pulled it open. Parked across the entrance of the cottage was a wooden cart. A chestnut brown horse stood tethered at its front. The horse lifted its head and looked at her for a brief moment and then returned to munching on a bucket of oats.

"Mademoiselle, your carriage awaits." As he spoke, Jimmy gave Rachel a deep bow.

Rachel clung to the seat of the cart as a jolt sent her left and a lurch flung her to the right. Each rock or pothole threatened to shake the cart into pieces.

"This is glorious, don't you think, Rachel." It was a statement, not a question. Any trace of stress and urgency Jimmy had shown the previous night was gone.

"Yeah, if you like being shaken to the bone." Rachel momentarily lost her grip of the seat as the cart rolled into a hole. First the front and then the back wheel dropped and lurched before it levelled itself. Rachel scrambled, trying to regain her grasp and tentative security.

"The open road." Jimmy gestured ahead.

"Dirt track," Rachel corrected. Jimmy ignored Rachel's comment and continued.

"Sunshine." He raised his hand to the sky, indicating the sun. Rachel couldn't deny the sun was shining, and it was very warm. She couldn't even claim a cloud.

"We've delicious provisions."

Okay, yes, the food *was* delicious.

"And the best company."

He smiled at Rachel. Jimmy had that annoying way of always seeing the bright side, and, most annoying of all, making her see the best in things. It was infectious and she was happy to be infected. She smiled back at him. On one side of the road was thick green forest and on the other fields of gold and lavender. It was beautiful and smelled delicious. She had to concede, despite the quality of the cart ride, they were having an adventure.

The sun had almost disappeared, leaving a smudge of orange lingering above the tree-tops, when Jimmy turned the cart into a clearing. A huge stone temple stood in front of them. It was dark and looming.

"This is where we'll be staying for the night. I've got a few friends who live here. They'll put us up."

"In the Acropolis?" Rachel laughed.

Jimmy pulled the horse's reigns to the left, directing the cart around the side. It seemed to Rachel the temple was miles long, but soon she could hear the sound of music and the chatter of multiple voices. Permeating the air was the smell of roasting meat. As they turned the corner, yet another immaculate garden lay in front of them. Fruit trees were scattered amongst a sea of colourful flowers and thick foliage bordered a wide path. Two figures strolled side by side, their heads close together in intense conversation. To the left, connected to the building with a covered portico, was a terrace that resembled an open-air drawing room. A small group of people were standing or lying on stone benches arranged around a fire. Figures were draped in white cloth, which hung from their bodies in elaborate folds. Intricate embroidery in red, blue and gold adorned the edges. A young man with a headful of dark curls was playing a soft tune on a lyre. Stars appeared, bright in the darkening sky, as the last of the sun faded. Rachel stood a step behind Jimmy as he stopped at the periphery of the gathering.

"Pothos, it isn't all about yearning and sexual desire. Love is kind, patient and loyal."

A slender youth rose from his seat and approached the older woman who'd been speaking. He touched his hand to his breast as he spoke.

"But the pleasure of yearning for your love object is so intense, so bittersweet. It's delicious."

"You forget, I know the cruelty and pain of being parted from the one I love."

"How could we forget, Demeter? It defines you."

"The love of a mother is uncond—"

"Unconditional. Yes, yes. You've told us. I think the

only love that truly matters is for oneself," interrupted another beautiful youth who was looking at himself in a hand mirror.

"How tiresome you are, Narcissus. But what have we here?" Pothos moved across the square towards Jimmy. He recognised him immediately and stepped forward, his arms outstretched.

"Jimmy. It's been such a long time, I've missed you." Pothos clasped Jimmy in his arms and held him tight. "And who is this beautiful creature?"

"Welcome, my dear." Demeter removed Rachel's hand from Pothos's grip. "You must be a friend of Jimmy's."

"We've only known each other a few weeks, but I guess so." Jimmy blushed. Demeter and Pothos exchanged glances.

"You see what I mean, Demeter? The sweet joy of longing."

"It's not like that at all." Rachel laughed, giving Jimmy a gentle push. Again, Jimmy blushed.

"Anyway, I'm dead, and we're on the way to the afterlife." All of the gods' eyes shifted to Jimmy.

"How can that be, Jimmy?" Demeter frowned.

"I'm doing Death a favour. He made a mistake and I'm just trying to fix it." Jimmy avoided Demeter's eye.

"Since when does Death make mistakes?"

Jimmy forced a laugh. "We're all human." He attempted another laugh at his own joke and turned away to pick up two goblets. "Wine, Rachel? You must be thirsty?"

Again, the gods looked at one another.

"You must be tired after your journey. We're being

rude. Will you join us for some refreshments? Sit, eat, drink." An array of dishes were paraded in front of her: roasted meats, olives, bread and fresh fruit. Rachel helped herself. Two figures who had been sitting quietly in the corner following the conversation now stood up. One of them addressed her.

"Don't you think love should be harmonious, Rachel?" He pulled his mane of hair away from his face.

"It never is. Even the people who should love you have their own agenda."

Anteros smiled and tilted his head, his hair falling, abundant, over one shoulder. "And if you could take your revenge on the people who didn't love you in the way you need, would you?"

Rachel stopped chewing and thought for a moment. "I'd like them to know how it feels to be pushed out and isolated." She looked to Jimmy, thinking of how his brother treated him, how her family treated her.

"What do you think, Jimmy?" Anteros switched his gaze to Jimmy.

"I don't know."

"Really?" Anteros urged.

Jimmy shuffled his feet. "I guess I think you can't punish someone for how they feel—or don't feel. But that's not the point, you're having the wrong argument—all types of love are embedded with fear, longing and grief—or it's not love. You're all saying that in your own way. I think loving someone is yours, it's how you feel, and whether it's returned or not isn't the point; it's not under control. Pain is part of that." Everyone was silent until Demeter moved forward and put her arms around Jimmy.

"Unconditional love," she murmured contentedly.

"If love is not equally matched on both sides, what's the point?" Anteros was insistent. Jimmy snorted. It was typical of the love gods to misunderstand. Shallow and blinkered, they could only see love from their own individual perspectives, but then that was their job, even if it was infuriating.

The second figure, who had yet to speak, stood up and took Jimmy's arm, walking him a few paces towards the entrance to the temple.

"What do you think, Albina?" asked Jimmy.

"Ill-fated lovers are the saddest of all. However much love is between them, circumstances are against them. Good night Jimmy, I shall return with the dawn."

Hidden behind a pillar, Jimmy watched as a golden slither trailed across the deep-blue hues of the night garden. Albina moved with grace, delicate swirls glowed behind her. She stopped, collected the light in both hands, and launched it into the air. A chink of orange appeared on the horizon to the east.

"It's okay, Jimmy, you can come out. I know you're there." He crept from behind the pillar and cautiously stepped into the emerging dawn. He tripped on the lyre that had been left the previous evening. Its strings called out as if in pain as it toppled over onto the ground. As he got close to her, she held out her hands and led him deeper into the garden and away from the temple.

"I know why you're here, Jimmy."

"You do?" Jimmy gulped.

"It's obvious you're in love with her, and you want my protection. You seek to stay together."

Jimmy nodded. "I didn't plan on falling in love with her but there you have it. Now I have and I need your help."

"The only way, legally speaking, is if she goes back to the mortal world and you continue on your path of defying Death and become mortal. As a human, you wouldn't be you, as you are now, and there's no guarantee you'd know each other, let alone be in love."

"No, I don't want that. I want Rachel to stay here. Isn't there some way to keep her here?"

"Not that I know of. I'm sorry, Jimmy."

Jimmy sat on a bench, folding his arms around his body. Albina sat down next to him. Together they watched as sunlight broke through the trees.

"He knows everything you've done, Jimmy. He's waiting for you to do the right thing. You know that, don't you?"

"I hate him. This is all his fault. He wouldn't let her stay and he doesn't understand that I'm capable of more. He wants me to do the 'right thing,' as you say, so he doesn't have the shame of having to send me down. That's all. This is all about him. As usual."

"He loves you, Jimmy, and he has such a lot on his shoulders."

Jimmy stood up and shouted, "You're supposed to be the Protector of Ill-Fated Lovers. You're supposed to help! But what good are you? You're as bad as he is." Tears rolled down Jimmy's face and dripped onto his robe.

"You're right, I'm sorry. Death is too powerful and

Rachel is here illegally. He will separate you in the end. I can offer some sanctuary, but not long term. I can get you some time to talk to the other love gods and find out if they have any solutions."

Rachel thought about what she'd heard as she crawled back through the bushes. The conversation about death didn't make any sense to her, and Jimmy was upset with his brother again. He'd also said he loved her. Rachel was surprised; it hadn't occurred to her. They were becoming good friends and she liked him, but love was not what she'd expected, not at all. When alive she wouldn't have liked him; he was far too awkward. But being in limbo had given her the chance to be herself, the person she was beneath all the nonsense and work of being alive, and Jimmy had been a large part of that. She was grateful to and fond of Jimmy; it was an unusual relationship she'd never experienced before. But she was sure it wasn't love. When alive she didn't have these problems because she didn't have these feelings.

Rachel didn't stand up until she reached the temple and was sure neither Jimmy nor Albina had seen her.

Pretending to be asleep, Rachel kept her arm over her face so Jimmy couldn't see her eyes as he re-entered the room. Pouring himself a goblet of wine, he dropped it, spilling it on his robe. The goblet clanked numerous times as it bounced on the stone floor. Rachel took advantage of his mistake and pretended to stir from her sleep, stretching her arms and sitting up. She rubbed her eyes to complete the façade.

"Sorry, sorry, sorry. Go back to sleep." Fumbling with a cloth to mop up the liquid, Jimmy was down on all fours.

"What on earth are you doing up at the crack of dawn?"

"I just needed a drink."

She was disappointed at his logical answer. He'd need drawing out. "You look upset. Is everything okay?"

He continued mopping. "Yes, why wouldn't it be? I'm just fed up with spilling things and falling over things and making a mess of everything." This was great. He was one step away from confession. Jimmy smiled.

"Well, not everything." He paused. "How would you feel about staying here a bit longer?"

"Everyone seems nice. Mostly. If a little love-obsessed. But why? I thought we were on our way to the other side."

"A change of plans."

"Another? You never tell me what's really going on. Besides, this is *my* death, and I don't think it's going so well. I had no idea it would be so complicated."

"I thought we were having a good time—an adventure." He slumped into a sitting position on the floor. He looked pitiful.

"Yes, I suppose, but I'm beginning to think it's all a bit fishy."

"Fishy?"

"I think you keep things from me, and that's not friendship in my book." Rachel thought that was a bit harsh and Jimmy looked sad, like a crumpled teacloth waiting to go into the washing machine, but she couldn't relent. He was quiet for a few minutes.

"Rachel, you know how I told you that you got killed by mistake?"

"Yes." She was puzzled.

"And that I was waiting to hear for orders as to what to do?"

"Yes."

"Well ..." He flinched, afraid of his confession.

"Jimmy, just spit it out."

"I killed you, and it was up to me to sort it out. I'm really, really sorry." Jimmy hid his face behind his enlarged hand.

"You killed me? How?" Now she was perplexed.

"I borrowed the Scythe from my brother, and instead of a panic attack, you ... died." He closed his eyes, waiting to be told off.

"Death's your brother!?"

"You've got two choices."

"Choices? I thought death was kind of final."

"Normally, yes, but officially Death didn't take you. I did, and it's not my job. Jules says I have to sort it out. So here we are."

"Death is called Jules?"

Two choices. If she decided to return to her life she would remember nothing of what had happened to her in limbo, and all her anxieties that had drifted away over the previous weeks would return.

Or, she could choose what was behind door number two and go with Death to the other side. But there was no knowing what was over there. Jimmy didn't know: not his department.

She was furious with him. Her death hadn't been a doctor's mistake but his mistake. And Death was his brother—no wonder he wasn't very flexible. But he'd also said to Albina that he loved her and was trying to find a way to keep them together. And he still hadn't revealed his true feelings about her.

Watching him, a pathetic lump slumped on the floor, made her anger subside. Feeling sorry for him meant she couldn't stay angry with him, even if he had lied about almost everything.

"You got me into this, Jimmy, and I think it's only fair you help me out of it." Rachel sat next to him, and gently stroked his shoulder. "Tell me everything about this place, who you are and what you do. I'm guessing you're not The Caretaker. Is there even such a thing?"

Jimmy shook his head. "I'm sorry, Rachel. I just wanted to do something more important and show Jules he could trust me and then ..." He trailed off.

"And then what?"

"It just got out of hand." He turned to her and for the first time looked her dead in the eyes. "Rachel, I need to show you what I really do."

The hall contained row upon row of small bell-shaped glass jars. Each jar had a square white label stuck on the front, displaying a name and date. It was dark; sporadic rays of light fell across the shelves where the curtains had holes and tears. Dust rotated in the air, catching the light and sparkling like glitter. Jimmy switched on the lights; they blinked on one after the other across the huge expansive ceiling.

"It's everyone's bad emotions, their anxiety and neg-ativity." Rachel followed him further into the room. She strained her neck trying to see how high the shelves were stacked.

"But there are so many of them."

"There are a lot of people. Everyone suffers from time to time to a greater or lesser extent, but mostly people live a benign existence. There has to be an adequate happy/sad balance in the universe and when you get a spike either way it skews that balance. Sadness and happiness are linked and a person's ability to lead a rewarding life means being able to experience a range of emotions. If a jar fills beyond a certain level and quantity, I step in."

"Step in?"

"Yeah, well, panic attacks, red mists, you know all too well what I mean. I manage the misery process. Some people can't deal with pain and pretend they're okay, so panic attacks are there to raise the stakes, push people into getting help. I've been seeing to you for a while now." He looked pleased.

"Thanks very much, but really there was no need."

"Oh, no problem." He realised he was actually enjoying explaining to her how his job worked. "While you're suf-fering, you feel like you're the only one, but clearly you're not. That's just ridiculous."

"Are you saying I'm ridiculous?" Rachel was hurt.

"No, never. It's just the way the process works. To avoid a contagion, the suffering is very much restricted to the individual. You can't see what's going on in someone else's mind." He quietly laughed.

"A personal service delivered just about anywhere."

"Yeah." Jimmy laughed louder. "People think they're alone in their misery. They think people won't understand, or that they're a bother, or worst of all, boring others with their problems. Look at the way your parents are with you. So sufferers never share their feelings, which then heightens them. It's up to each individual to seek help. You know, you have to want to get better. It's a cycle. Good, isn't it?" He was beaming at her.

"I don't think 'good' is quite the right word," Rachel scolded.

"No, you're quite right, sorry. It's not good. It's clever."

"Clever but cruel." She turned away from him and walked along the rows of shelves, trailing her hand across the dusty jars. It was clever, and the balance had been maintained because of him. He'd done a good job as long as humans had suffered, and that was as long as they'd existed. The nature and cause of suffering may have changed through time, but it invariably ended up the same way: with insecurity and anxiety, fear and depression, panic, confusion and loneliness. Suffering had a long list of symptoms and Jimmy was the master of maintaining them all.

"But what about me, then? Where are my jars?"

He led her to the back of the storage facility. There were four doors. He approached the one on the far right.

"These cases are currently active." Pulling out an enormous bunch of keys from the pocket of his robe, he fumbled with the key ring until he found the correct one and unlocked the door. This room was smaller and cleaner, the jars were brightly coloured and completely full. He led her around a corner into an alcove. There were four shelves filled with jars that were labelled with her name.

"There are loads of them, I had no idea ... but look at them, what does it mean?" She took a jar down from the shelf and read the label: *Rachel Stone: 1994, Parents break up*. She read the next one: *Father moves to Australia*; the next one: *Mother remarries*; the next one: *Birth of half-brother*; and the final one: *2000, Abortion*.

Rachel was stunned.

"What does this ... please, I don't understand." She was sobbing.

"Your panic attacks, your sense of hopelessness, what do you think caused them?"

"I'm not well, I'm ill, I'm going to ... I'm dead ..."

"By accident."

"Yes, but, crowded places, they're hot, all those people, anything could happen."

"Not everyone feels like that in seedy night spots, unbelievable as it sounds."

"You're lying! I love my family, and the abortion was the right thing to do." Tears were running down her face. She wiped her nose on her sleeve.

"That may be true, but it's not that simple. Human emotion is complex."

"How the hell do you know? You're not even human."

"But I know you, Rachel. You pretend to be tough but you've been through all these horrible things and never allowed yourself to be sad or even given yourself a break."

Rachel slipped to the ground in a crumpled mass. What he said was true. Her fear had become a mask for her grief. Fear of accidents and disaster were a deflection from her disappointments and sadness. Jimmy sat beside her. Snot ran from her nose like two veins of lava. She whimpered.

"I thought being successful and in control would protect me from pain, but I can't get away from it anywhere. I'm better off dead."

"I wouldn't want you to die."

"You killed me."

"That was then. You could have a great life, Rachel, if only you could see that everything is okay. You're enough."

"But everything is always so hard all of the time. I've struggled for everything I've got, everything I've achieved, clamouring, determined to be slimmer, cleverer, more exciting, more accomplished, just better than I actually am. Desperate to show everyone how perfect I can be." Once again Rachel sobbed.

"I don't want to sound smug ..."

"Then don't," she snapped through a sniff.

"But you've been happy here, I think."

"I'm dead, that doesn't count."

"You've been happy because you haven't had to try. We've played games, travelled, enjoyed—" He wanted to say being together but continued with "—nature and good food. We've just been living. And it's been good, great even."

Her sobs subsided and she stared at him. "So I'm better off here, dead."

"Except you're not actually dead. You still have a chance to live."

"Why can't I stay here?"

"It's against the rules. You're not a god or associated being."

"Okay then. If I really have to choose, I want to know what Death is like. I want to see him."

"Why on earth? You know what he'd do. To both of us."

"I've got nothing to lose, have I? It might make it easier to, you know, make a decision."

"You can't look Death in the eye and come away the same person, he's very imposing if you're not used to it, I don't …"

"Jimmy, please." She touched his hand. Jimmy gave a small shiver as the touch went through him.

"There's one thing we could do."

"What?"

"He has a nap at three every afternoon."

"A nap?"

"We'd have to be really quiet, and quick. In and out, like lightning."

Death's bedroom was cosy, wood-panelled and dominated by a huge, canopied four-poster bed. Rachel guessed Tudor. The curtains and furnishings were matching, expensive, red velvet. A large stuffed raven, wings outstretched, kept guard above the bed. Rachel and Jimmy hovered behind the heavy oak door, attempting to see through the gap between the door and its frame.

"He's really into home design, every room is from a

different period of history. He says decorating helps him to relax and takes his mind off things."

"I wish it helped me."

"It's never the same when you do something for a living." He shrugged his shoulders at her. "He's asleep." Death was snoring so loudly that each time he exhaled, the glass on his bedside shook. His mouth hung open.

"I can see the family resemblance. He's sort of handsome, despite the loose jaw."

Jimmy frowned. "Really? Thanks, I think."

He tentatively pushed the door open. It squeaked. He froze. Death stirred, and turned over. "Quick, go and look at him, then let's get out of here."

Rachel stepped out from behind Jimmy, slowly placing her foot gently on the thick carpet. She approached the bed and stopped a few feet away from his head.

"Not too close." Jimmy hissed a warning. Rachel kept going and shook Death by the arm.

"No! Rachel, stop!" He ran forward and pulled her away. In her confusion, her foot caught and tangled on the bottom of his robe. She lurched forward, Jimmy automatically holding out his hand to catch her. But her momentum was too strong and she fell forward onto her face, squealing in pain as Jimmy landed on top of her. Jimmy accidentally leant on her arm.

"Ouch, Jimmy, be bloody careful."

Death, slowly rising up from the bed, expanded his form as if a bird of prey spreading its wings. He filled the room. Booming, he shouted, staring down at the confused mass on the floor, "What is going on here?" The glass in the window frame shook. He glowered at Jimmy struggling on the floor, tangled in arms and legs and clothes and hair. And Rachel crushed beneath him.

Jimmy stood up; Rachel followed, taking refuge behind him. Death was irate and their performance wasn't helping.

"Do you think you are The Two Stooges?"

"I think you'll find there were three—" Jimmy regretted his interruption immediately.

"Be quiet! James, you've defied me one too many times." Death maintained his engorged body.

Rachel stepped forward, keeping her eyes lowered. "It wasn't Jimmy's fault, it was mine. I made him bring me here. He didn't know my intention to wake you. I'm really sorry, but please don't blame Jimmy. He was just trying to make things easier on me."

Death was confused; he looked at Rachel and then at Jimmy.

"Is this true, James?"

"No, it was my idea. I thought it would help her choose." He stepped in front of Rachel, pushing his chest out.

"Don't do this, Jimmy. It was my fault. Please believe me." Rachel pulled at his shoulder to get in front.

"You two are as bad as each other. If, as you say Rachel, this is your fault then I've no choice."

"No, please, Jules. I don't want her to die."

Death shook his head at Jimmy. He turned to Rachel, ready to complete his promise.

In a panic, she shouted, "I don't want to die either. I want to go back. Jimmy may have made some terrible decisions but he's helped me to understand my problems and shown me that life doesn't always have to be a miserable struggle. I get it now." Her voiced calmed. "Life's not perfect. It's beautiful but it's not perfect. And that mess and ugliness, that pain and confusion, heightens all that is good. When life's a mess, the best way to solve it is not through perfection. Or using death to avoid it." She turned to Jimmy.

"Jimmy, you're an incredible person and I hope you can believe that about yourself too. You are perfect the way you are. And you have beautiful hands." Rachel slipped her hands into Jimmy's and kissed his enlarged knuckles. "Even this one."

As usual, Jimmy blushed, but beneath the red his relief made him feel as if he could stand up straight after years of carrying his worries on his back. Rachel continued. "I love you, Jimmy. You've made me happy. But I must face my fears and hopefully that means we won't see each other again. If I'm well, that is." Jimmy clasped her by the shoulders. The weight once again pressed on him.

"Don't go, please. I'll come with you, I'll become a mortal and find you."

"Amongst seven billion people." Death reminded him dryly, now back to his normal size.

"No, Jimmy, we both need to live. You're good at what you do and the universe needs you. I'm going to live the best life I can and maybe I'll see you in a few decades. Maybe then we can have something together."

He wanted to cry and stamp his feet but instead he clasped Rachel, holding her in a tight embrace. Anger gave way to contentment and slowly conceded to sadness.

It paralysed him. At last, he'd got what he wanted and she loved him, but she had chosen life. That was what he wanted for her, but not without him. He wasn't sure if he could ever forgive her.

Death wiped away the tear that rolled down his face to the bottom of his chin.

———◦◦◦———

Rachel sank backwards into the leather sofa, and it consumed her, sucking her in. A drunken couple fell across her, kissing with wide mouths and visible tongues. Her ears flinched at each beat of the music; it merged with the sounds of human exhilaration into silence. The couple became an indistinguishable outline, blending and fading into blackness. Rachel's body lost power. She tried to stand but fell to the floor. Crawling forward, she grasped onto a pair of legs. Jimmy lifted his hand, taking it away from the top of her head. After a moment's pause, he leaned forward and lovingly kissed her on the cheek. That was the last time he'd visit her. It would be too painful otherwise. That's what his love demanded from him. Besides, he was sure she'd now have the strength to get help.

He looked around the bar and walked through the room to sit next to a toned and tanned man in his early twenties. His group of friends were all laughing and swigging from pint glasses. Jimmy placed his hand on the man's head and whispered:

"It won't be obvious now, but at some point you'll understand that I'm helping you."

—◆—

"It sounds as if you've been experiencing a high level of anxiety for a prolonged period." The psychologist leaned forward, offering Rachel a tissue. "What do you think made you realise you need help?"

Rachel licked the flow of tears from her top lip. She attempted to speak, but the sound constricted in her throat.

"Take your time."

"I ... I don't know. It doesn't seem normal for someone of my age to worry so much about everything."

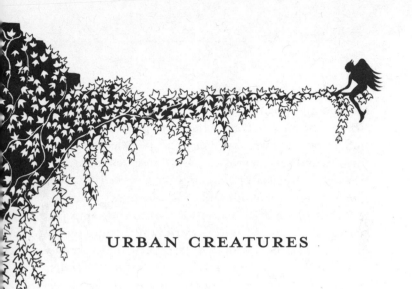

URBAN CREATURES

Have you ever thought about the creatures that migrate to London, Margot? What do you think they're looking for? Do you think they find it? Awful rain tonight, black windows and condensation, I can't see out. People say it always rains in England, but it's mainly a miserable covering of grey cloud. Moderate and predictable. Like the English character. Not in '39, of course, our finest hour, my finest hour. Five months and a dozen trips to London. I'll be through the suburbs soon. *Haringey, Hornsey, Potters Bar.* I'm used to this yo-yoing back and forth now. But I'm not used to being without you. Or her.

Seven hours still to Newcastle. Home is supposed to be sweet.

You'll be waiting for me at the station. I don't know what I'll tell you, Margot. You said not knowing would be the worst. I agreed with you, at first. That evening we'd been delayed driving back home. Snow, the roads were hard going. Northumbrian weather can be dangerous. When we found out, an image kept playing out in my mind, over and over. I saw her pacing forward and back, forward and back in a windowless room, searching for a way out. *The longer she's missing, the less likely we are to find her*, Sergeant Smith said.

Was it my fault? I insisted we go to the cabin that weekend. There was no reason not to trust her on her own. She was angry, said we interfered with her studies. *What do we do now?* I asked Sergeant Smith. *Wait when she could still be alive?* Vera's mum said Connie hadn't been over that Saturday night. By then it was already night, Sunday night, and she'd been gone for twenty-four hours. *Try not to worry*, Sergeant Smith said, *It's probably a boy, usually is.* A boy—our Connie! *Leave it to us*, he said. But I *had* to do something, you know that, don't you Margot. I tried to approach her disappearance the way I did everything: methodically. Each possibility isolated and tested until the cause was found and the solution reached. Telephoned Julia. It rang but no answer. Mother, Beatrice and Edith. School friends. Even her piano teacher. That Sunday night was the first time I saw you panic. A struggle taking place in your eyes, imperceptible to anyone else. Beautiful blue, you and Connie both, bluebell eyes. Even at Bletchley we were calm. Neither of us knew what the other did. We fell in love on superficial facts and jaunts into the countryside. Tall poppy grass, paste sandwiches and flasks of tea. Chemistry too. I couldn't have guessed you were from the North East, not with your BBC accent. You said, *When this is over, I want to make head teacher by the time I'm forty.* Career came first, you made that clear enough. Too late to be rational, I was already in love. Still am, Margot. I tell you that. I'll tell you that again. *A girl matching your Connie's description bought a ticket for London at approximately 7:30 Saturday night. We believe she boarded the 20:13 overnight train to London,* said Sergeant Smith. She wasn't dead; we could live again. I followed her to London the next day, first train. Pale complexion and strawberry blonde, your icy demeanour and symmetrical face made it impossible to think you could laugh. Yet you laugh at anything, instant guffaws and grins. Connie's the same. *Bonnie Connie*, I called her. You didn't like that and you'd say, *Her name is Constance.* Slowly. Emphasising each syllable. You did the same when I wanted you to be my Margie—*My name is Margot.* I understand, you want to keep your identity. In the same way, one child was enough for you. I wanted to thrive amongst a brood, living in a house brimming with children and a baby to dote on. But your happiness was more important. *Do you have any idea where the lass was headed for?* Sergeant Smith asked.

I tried to write you a letter from the bedsit I rented, testing out the words, seeing how they sounded. Boom and whoosh, a hiss of gas under a single bulb and a lilac Candlewick counterpane. The words were all wrong on the page, wrong in my mind. So I sit here on the train, scared.

I'm scared, Margot. Knowing is the worst.

The UK is the third nuclear state—don't you think that's wrong, Dad? She didn't want me to go with her, to the protest. Recoiled, actually recoiled, at us going together. I wouldn't let her go alone. She never understood I agreed with her. CND posters on every wall—not so long ago it was *She loves you, yeah, yeah, yeah.* They look clean cut compared to how they look now. Long hair and judgment. The summer of love changed everything. After the protest I thought she might come back; just a weekend away. *Have you seen this girl?* A hundred faces, blank. No word. Until now. Pressure, Margot, did we put too much pressure on her to achieve? Qualifications, university applications, future prospects. We couldn't tell her what we did in the war. Official Secrets Act. Best work of our lives. We met the challenge. CND is her fight. Nothing to do with us, nor our generation, she believed. *You can act when you're finished at university—a good engineering brain shouldn't go to waste. You take after me,* I said. Rolled her eyes at our similarity. Alan Turing invited us to join his team. Shortened the war by six months. Ten machines, all decrypting messages for D-Day. I can't tell you that, Margot, and I can't tell Connie. I want her to understand. We were the first, Alan and the team, to use valves, revolutionised electronics. We did amazing things. Maybe if I could have told her how innovative our work was, how crucial, she'd understand and listen to what I was trying to tell her. She might have stayed. The misunderstanding between us was too great. Did we push her too hard? Remember the theatre group, she couldn't stop talking about it. Raising money for CND, bringing the message of peace, love and mutually assured destruction. Enthralled, I'd say she was. I didn't take it seriously—didn't hear her need. We were fighting for something important, maybe that's what she wants to do, in her own way, in her own time. Communism, Korea and Vietnam. Drugs, sexual revolution and the rat race. It's all changed. Tradition doesn't work for the young generation. She thinks the establishment preserves its own and sends the poor to their deaths. But she doesn't understand, our war was for everyone. We had free love: it was called the fear of death and no tomorrow. How does she see us, Margot? Boring and safe, happily so. It's not how I see us. I struggled hard to get my degree, evening classes weren't easy, and I was the first in my family to go to university. Does my Connie understand that? We've given her everything she needs and she's gone beyond us. A different species.

A nice cup, dark brown and hot, makes a change. *Bun or roll, ham or cheese?* Bun looks stale. Still raining. Cheese roll looks the least unappealing. Tea, food and flyers. That's been life for the past five months. I almost wish it still were; at least in uncertainty there's hope. *Have you seen this girl? At least take a flyer. Have you seen this girl? No? Peace to you too, young man. Have you seen this girl? Are you sure? Look again. Maybe? Please, please tell me where.* Maybe I shouldn't have looked so hard.

I can't make this right, Margot. I could show you and then you'd believe. Bluebell eyes. That's how I knew. They thought she'd gone back home. *It was a shame,* he said, *she was a talented performer. Worked hard too, believed in the cause and sharing the message of peace. An asset to the theatre group.* I should have known. The church had mostly been destroyed. Only two walls partially stand-ing. Windows shattered. Any congregation long gone. One hundred and twenty-three churches were bombed during the war. That's why they use the church hall to rehearse—free. He seemed sorry, the young man, sorry she'd gone.

Don't look at me, don't see me. Too late. *A business trip. Yes, it went well, thank you for asking. No, no news. None that I can tell you, anyway.* They mean well, the neighbours, but the pity in their eyes, I can't stand it. And his kids are safe at home. For Christ's sake, I hope I don't see anyone else I know. You wanted to go home, to the place you grew up, Margot. It made sense. Newcastle, a new university in a burgeoning city where I could work too. Goodbye to London and my development work at the telephone exchange. Paying for this bunk was a waste, I can never sleep. My mind's travelling ahead of the train.

What to tell you?

The rain has stopped now, the window clear of con-densation and I can see the moon, a delicate silver slither. Beautiful. She's staring at me, Phoebe. Phoebe—the eye of night, my grandfather used to call her. It was meant as a comfort. But what she has revealed is devastating. I think she commands these creatures. I think it's her world. We waited for Connie, a late child. You wanted to be established, so you could return to work. And you did it, a mother returning to work. It was unheard of, but not for you. Brave and bold with bluebell eyes. Just like Connie. She was never afraid to perform. Do you remember, Margot? From a toddler she would sing and dance when I played the piano. Connie loved the moon. She said its beams were magical. There's no pity in Phoebe tonight—she is brazen, shining her light. The night I found her, I saw a silhouette against the moon, a full moon large and low. A perfect silhouette, Margot, of a fox, slender and sleek, sitting in the window frame of the bombed-out church. It jumped down. I stopped and stared. It sat and gazed into my eyes, human in its enquiry of me. Blue eyes, it had bluebell eyes. A blue shadow, a moonlight shadow, stretched in front of the creature. I saw it. I saw it was the shadow of a girl, our girl.

Are all urban creatures captives of the moon? Lost children, did they somehow transgress or fail to keep a bargain? Is that why Phoebe took her? Their cries are terrifying. Lonely, they sound lonely. Is that possible, or just my human fear? Dawn soon, Phoebe's secrets kept for another night. What can I tell you, Margot? Can the lost return to us in the morning light? Do they even want to? I can't make this right, fix it and bring her back. I fix things, Margot, I work problems till I find a solution. I build machines, machines to make the world right. Is there a machine that can bring her back?

She's lost, Margot, lost to us. That's what I'll tell you, and it's not a lie. Sometimes, no matter what we do, we're fighting alone; we become lost to one another. I will tell you she has disappeared, but I will pray to the moon to relinquish her and bring her back into the light of day.

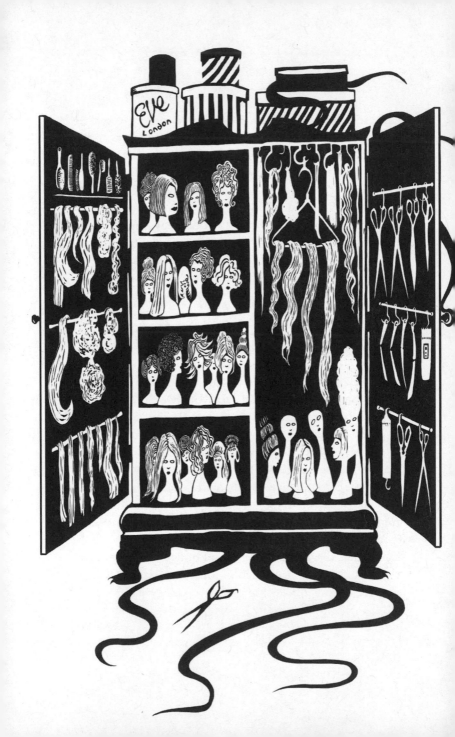

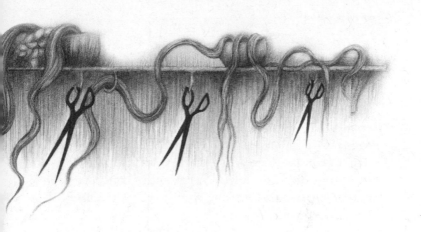

CROWNING GLORY

The razor has to be sharp. There can be no fumbling, no confusion, it has to be quick. Precise. The high ponytail or plait the most convenient; one clean action, it's all bundled up for you—what better? Get the hair band as well: one doesn't want to lose any at the crucial moment.

Angela stood on the escalator, surveying the heads of her fellow commuters.

She's just about perfect. A lovely thick bunch, beautiful chestnut, like Freddie. What a wonderful ride he was, powerful and strong. Such a shame about his broken leg. Daddy was wrong, she was being careful. Public places are a must. The Underground provides a great vantage point; you could stare at the top of someone's head all day long and they'd never have a clue. Marvellous. Cafés and museums can work, though one has to be more careful. Even the street has its benefits. But two rules have to be adhered to at all times: the exit must be clear, and only strangers. The risks are higher if you covet the familiar. Military training is desirable, not essential. Having said that, of course, there are no fixed rules, just principles: remain flexible and seize opportunities. Angela was a master and had no formal training at all, just a surfeit of commitment and fortitude.

There were two ways Angela pursued her hobby—both had risks. This public method carried more dangers but was accompanied by a delightful thrill. The other route was enjoyable and private, but sordid: drugging women who sold themselves and taking more than they were offering. However, she compensated them well. Money does speak the loudest. Today, Angela was in need of exhilaration. She raised her hand and allowed it to hover a millimetre over the hair of a young woman who stood directly before her on the escalator. For the briefest of moments the tips of her fingers skimmed the maze of curls. As the woman stepped forward onto the motionless ground, Angela pulled the cut-throat razor from her inside pocket and with one swift action she separated hair from owner. Pushing the plait deep into her pocket, she darted forward, moving fast, absorbed into the protection of the crowd.

"You're a real early bird this morning," Sasha said as she grinned at Angela, advancing across the office towards her. A young woman followed behind, running occasionally to catch up.

Smile and wave, Angela, smile and wave. Just like the Queen.

"Yes, absolutely." Angela forced her mouth to match the shape of Sasha's. The Queen, truly an example to us all, in control and serene, giving the appearance of gliding through life, yet fulfilling the most difficult of roles, dedicated to public service. These young girls didn't know the meaning of giving oneself over to the needs of your country.

"This is Harjeevan, she'll be working alongside me." Harjeevan stepped out from behind Sasha, her petite hand held directly out in front of her, the thumb sticking straight up at a ninety-degree angle to her fingers. Angela stared. Sasha was embarrassed. "You did remember we had a new member of staff starting today?" Angela continued to stare. The girl had the most glorious hair. It was thick, dark and long, stopping barely an inch above her buttocks. Angela expelled a short, sharp, loud laugh. Those roots were unlike any she'd ever seen ... full head coverage. She swallowed her excess saliva.

"Yes, of course, forgive me. I can honestly say it's an absolute pleasure to meet you." She gripped Harjeevan's hand and held it firm. Harjeevan giggled and lowered her eyes. Angela maintained her grasp. Harjeevan attempted to retrieve her blood-starved fingers and looked up at Angela for mercy. She stared back. Angela watched the girl's eyes as they followed her hairline. *She must know,* Angela thought. *She can see as well as I can the quality of a woman's crowning glory.*

"Angela is one of our senior inspectors—if there's anyone dodging tax, Angela sniffs them out." Sasha forced a laugh. Angela continued gazing at Harjeevan, unwilling to be distracted.

"I hate to break this up, but I think we'd better get on and show Harjeevan where she'll be working."

"Yes, yes, that's what we're here for. Oh, and the joy of social interaction." Angela looked directly at Sasha, then turned again to Harjeevan. "I'll have plenty of time to get to know Harjeevan, I should think."

Sasha laughed again, leading her assistant away. Angela watched them. They walked with relaxed bodies, completely at ease, talking, turning to each other, their shoulders shaking with laughter.

"She might be okay, if only she'd take that pole out of her arse. Good thing the old bag's heading for retirement." That's what Janine had said, the little chav—one step above inherent baseness, and her hair a pathetic clump of greasy spikes. Angela couldn't be sure if they were actually talking about her. They'd all stopped speaking, pretending to get on with some work, as she'd emerged from around the corner. How could she legitimately make their lives a waking nightmare without sufficient evidence? They were sloppy with their careless talk but not sloppy enough.

"Hey, how are you?"

"Oh, Harjeevan, you shocked me. I was in a world of my own." *Nice tight plait … look at the girth … magnificent.* "How are you settling in? Everything to your liking, I trust?"

"Fantastic, everything's great. Sasha's lovely to work for and everyone's been so kind—do you really want your tea that strong?"

"Er, oh yes, I see what you mean. I seem to have squashed the life out of the pitiful thing." Angela lifted the teabag from her cup and squeezed herself behind Harjeevan, lightly brushing against her back. As she moved past, towards the bin, she very gently traced her forefinger down the spine of the plait. She shivered with delight and plopped the deflated teabag into the bin.

"A few of us are going for lunch. You know, to celebrate the end of my first week ... do you fancy coming along?"

"I see. The ladies that lunch of the Inland Revenue, how ... cosy. Yes, I'd love to. Thank you for the invitation."

Pizza, wonderful. A doughy mass with the nutritional value of a cardboard box. At least she didn't have to sit through hour upon hour of variety performances year after year—that's endurance for you—not to mention the interminable speeches at every ribbon-cutting event. The odd fast-food meal, she supposed, wouldn't do any irreparable damage. However, she wasn't so sure about the conversation. *It's fascinating the extent to which the love lives of those one has never met, and likely never will, can dominate the minds of these young women.* Angela imagined this must be how the Queen had felt on facing the 'Diana Problem.' Diana and her head-tilting manipulation of a society obsessed with beauty and youth. As far as Angela was concerned, Diana suffered from nothing more than a bad dose of 'poor me' syndrome. Such a bad influence on her children, she should be ashamed—if she had lived, of course.

"Harjeevan, dear, why don't you sit next to me?"

"Harjeevan can sit where she wants, Angela."

"No, it's fine, Sash, I'd love to sit with Angela. She's been at the office for the longest time, I can pick up a few tips."

"Quite." Angela was sure of it.

"So you were saying that only a small percentage of the hair sold in the UK is actually 'temple hair'?" Angela was leaning in close to Harjeevan, her eyes wide and fixed on the girl. She held her breath.

"Yeah, it's a real human rights issue. Some women are made to shave their heads by their husbands, while others are physically attacked, their hair taken by force." Harjeevan was flushed. "Sorry, I get really upset by it. These bloody WAGs have no idea; they think it's sacred or something. I could rip it off their ignorant heads."

"Yes, dear, I know exactly what you mean ... I would hate to see your beautiful hair come to such a fate." Angela smiled, cocking her head and slightly raising her eyebrows. She tugged gently on the bottom of Harjeevan's plait. Harjeevan covered her mouth as if she'd been burned with hot food.

"I'm so sorry ... talking about hair ... I'm such an idiot." She contorted her bottom lip, as she struggled to stop her gaze roaming upwards to scrutinise Angela's hairline.

"I'm not sure what you mean, darling." So, she knew. Angela supposed it was inevitable, but she wouldn't become downcast. She would be sure to get what she needed from this arrangement. Harjeevan excused herself and left the table, apologising as she rose. Despite the girl's faux pas, Angela was taken with her passionate outburst. How perfectly sublime: they shared a hobby. This would be easier than Angela had initially anticipated.

Angela loved her journey home. Nothing was quite as revitalising as the opportunities public spaces offered. Friday evening usually presented the pleasurable prospect of two unrestrained days of observing, waiting. But the thought of being absent from Harjeevan—or, more exactly, her hair—for a full forty-eight hours left Angela with a sense of restlessness and an unfamiliar lack of focus.

"Have a great weekend, Angela," Harjeevan's voice interjected from behind. Angela turned to see Harjeevan crossing the road with a buoyant trot. The surprise brought Angela to a standstill, her face becoming increasingly hot as she watched the girl reach the other side.

"Oh yes, Harjeevan, you too." Harjeevan waved, a small, happy wave, which contained the promise of a relaxed, carefree weekend. She broke into a delicate canter for a few short steps, causing her heavy plait to swing behind her.

Angela had mastered her jealousy of other women's assets long ago, but what still stung was suddenly being faced with another woman unashamed of her deficiency. How could she leave the house brazenly exhibiting her failure to the world? Had she no self-respect? A woman, no longer young, with a gentle sag in her cheeks and the barest covering of red fluff, sat next to Angela. Her scalp shone under the bright, artificial lighting of the tube carriage. Angela could never do that. She would not publicly accept her private humiliation. Getting up, she moved further down the train. Angela chose her new seat with care; stumbling across shopping bags and pushing through commuters, she seated herself next to a woman with luxuriant blonde locks. Not only gentlemen prefer blondes, she laughed to herself. But after a few moments, Angela admitted that, although ample and golden, the woman's hair just wasn't doing the trick. It wasn't Harjeevan's.

The blue neon lights lent the room a luminous glow and a bright halo circled the girl's raven head. Angela stood behind the girl, who sat in an upright wooden chair set in the centre of the room. Her legs were spread open and her knees created sharp right angles because the heels of her boots were so high. Her hair hung over the back of the chair—it was beautiful, dark and sleek. Angela poured powder into a champagne flute; bubbles fizzed to the surface as the substance made contact with the liquid. It only took a few moments to dissolve and would be just as quick to take effect. Angela walked around the chair and handed the girl the glass.

"Champers. You know how to treat a girl right." She giggled.

"Have as much as you want, my dear." Angela smiled down on her. "Drink up."

The girl gulped the champagne without stopping to breathe. By the time she'd finished the glass, her eyelids were drooping and she struggled to hold her head up.

"Don't fight it. Just sleep and it will all be over." Angela removed the razor from her bag and returned to stand behind the girl. She slid her hand under the hair and let it slither through her fingers. Divine. She shuddered. Gathering the hair and gripping it with one hand, she started to slice with the other. As the first few strands fell into her hand, she lost power in her limbs and her stomach became heavy. This didn't feel right. She held the cut hair in her fist and pushed her fingers into the strands. It was smooth, but a little too fine. Angela remembered Harjeevan trotting across the road, her mane of hair swinging with each step. Angela pushed a bundle of notes into the girl's bodice and left the room.

Harjeevan was already ten minutes late. Angela feared she wouldn't come and felt an ache of longing at the thought of having to wait yet another weekend. Pulling back the heavy lace curtain, she stretched her neck to look as far down the street as possible without causing herself injury. Angela's stomach lurched as she saw the girl turn the corner into her street. Damn, her hair was loose. The wind blew it against Harjeevan's face; she fought to push it back. *Never mind, we must endure.* The risk was worth it. Everything was ready. She'd made a proper dinner: roast beef and Yorkshire pudding, lots of greens. Apple crumble for dessert. Delicious. And plenty of wine, with added sedative.

The departure from her usual tactics broke all her rules (principles, she corrected herself) but she wanted that hair. Angela poured herself a small glass of sherry, toasted the Queen—who peered down from above the fireplace—and gulped the liquid in one movement. The doorbell rang. Angela patted the curls of her beautifully coiffured wig. The Queen had allowed her own hair to turn silver, but Angela wasn't as brave; she wanted to keep hers honey for a while longer. Satisfied at her appearance, she smoothed her clothes and answered the door.

"So sorry I'm late ... the bus ... you know." Harjeevan handed Angela a bottle of wine.

"I understand perfectly, my dear. Beaujolais, how lovely." *Could be worse. At least it's drinkable.* Angela led Harjeevan through her hallway. The walls were covered in pictures of glamorous young women with horses. Angela had cut them out of magazines and they were now so old they were yellowing at the corners, but the girls kept on smiling. It gave Angela no end of comfort. Harjeevan stared.

"You obviously like horses."

"Oh yes, dear, such fine animals. Beautiful manes." Angela gestured towards the door with a flat hand, indicating that Harjeevan should move through into the living room. "Would you like a glass of wine?"

"Yes, please. I don't usually, but ..."

"No need to explain, my dear, we are friends. Do take a seat in the living room." Angela grinned and made her way to the kitchen.

Harjeevan was surrounded. Hundreds of framed pictures of the Queen hung from every wall: the Queen on walkabout, the Queen posing in her finery, the Queen in uniform, on and off a horse, the Queen as a bride and the Queen as a child, the Queen with her own children. The Queen stared from all angles. Only one photograph wasn't of Her Majesty. Returning from the kitchen, Angela stopped in the living room doorway and watched as Harjeevan shifted her attention away from the plethora of queens. Set in the centre of a long sideboard, placed on a lace doily, the photograph was dominated by a middle-aged man holding a pipe in one hand, his other arm draped over the shoulders of a young woman. They were both smiling at the camera. The woman looked about twenty and was beautiful, stunningly so. Dressed in bright colours, her white-blonde hair reached down to her waist.

"That's my father." Angela handed Harjeevan the glass of wine.

"And who's the woman?" Harjeevan took a mouthful of wine.

"That's me." Harjeevan choked. "I know, it's hard to believe. It was taken a few months before Daddy died. Are you all right, my dear?" Still short of breath, Harjeevan nodded. "I was due to go back for my final year at university." Angela picked up the photograph and traced her finger over her former self. "Never mind. Shall we eat?"

"More wine?" Angela held the bottle over her guest's glass. The heavy meal had slowed the sedative's progress.

"Really, I've had enough." *She must have more, it's nearly time.*

"I can't have you thinking I'm not the perfect hostess. I tend towards excess. One can't do too much for an esteemed guest." Before Harjeevan could protest, Angela

Angela opened the doors of her large oak wardrobe. She gazed at the hundreds of bunches of human hair hanging in front of her, all perfectly packaged in clear plastic sheaths. She ran her hand along the row then slipped her fingers into a packet of bright auburn hair. She shuddered with excitement. A row of plastic heads wore exquisitely crafted wigs, in a variety of styles. Angela had a deal with a Bond Street wig maker. She paid for their discretion, and loyalty was important to both parties. *Enough.* Turning to the inner side of the door, she pulled a pair of scissors from a canvas holder. There were dozens of pairs. Trying the action of the scissors, she opened and closed the blades. Excellent, smooth movement, but too short. Replacing them, she chose another pair. These had long, thin, shining blades and she snipped them at the air. Perfect. She closed the wardrobe, walked to the mirror and reapplied her lipstick.

"Sorry to keep you."

Harjeevan was still awake—barely. She was putting up a valiant battle. Angela stopped behind her. Once again she arranged the girl's hair on her back. Two cuts at most. Raising the scissors, she slipped the blade under her hair at the base of her hairline. Harjeevan flinched, waving her hand about her head as if to brush away a fly. Angela grabbed her head.

"You young girls don't seem to understand the joy and nobility of the Queen. Look at her, go on, really look." As she closed the scissors, one side of Harjeevan's hair fell to the ground. The girl jerked her head, fighting to stay conscious. Adrenalin won through.

"What are you doing?" Turning enough to see the scissors, Harjeevan screamed. "What the hell? Get off! Get the fuck away!" She saw the hair on the floor, and frantically felt her head. Angela walked forward.

"Don't struggle, dear, I'm not going to hurt you. And there's no need to be vulgar." Harjeevan backed away. Angela stood between her and the exit, holding the scissors poised to complete their mission. Keeping her eyes towards Angela, Harjeevan groped sideways, her flailing hands connecting with the Queen above the fireplace. Heavier than she'd expected, it dropped. Harjeevan staggered towards the sideboard and launched the first thing she laid her hand on—the Queen in full military regalia, sitting proudly on her beautiful mare, sliced through the air and caught Angela on the corner of her eye. Harjeevan lunged forward, forcing Angela to the ground. The scissors were knocked from her hand. Attempting to break her fall, Angela snatched at anything, finally catching hold of the tablecloth. The cloth slid from the tabletop; china and glass rained down onto her. She was covered in a combination of gravy, Brussels sprouts and apple crumble. Her wig went awry, exposing a full head of thick grey hair. Harjeevan stood still, her mouth hanging open. Angela burst into tears.

"I lost my father, I lost my hair, but next time it happens nobody will laugh at me—I'm already prepared!" She endeavoured to straighten her wig as she screamed and cried, drumming her fists into the floor and kicking. Snot mingled with the food products. For a few moments

Harjeevan watched Angela's childish display. Satisfied she was in control, she bent down and gathered her hair into a bunch.

"This," Harjeevan shook her dislocated tresses in front of Angela's contorted face, "belongs to me."

"Love the haircut, Harj—give us a twirl." Sasha admired her assistant as she spun in front of her. "Didn't know you were fed up with your long locks, but a bob suits you."

"Thanks. It wasn't planned, I just fancied a change. You know how it is sometimes." She sat down at her desk. Janine rushed over.

"Have you heard the news? It's the best."

"What news?"

"Stop gossiping, Janine, and get back to work." Sasha waved Janine away.

"It's Angela. She won't be coming back. She's been signed off sick—indefinitely."

"That's sad," Harjeevan reflected. "I'm actually sorry … though I didn't know her that long." Harjeevan plunged her hand into her pocket and gripped her plait. She dug her fingers into the hair, working them into its centre, and rubbed the strands between her thumb and forefinger. She'd rubbed it so much for the past twenty-four hours that she'd worn away the braid until the hair frayed. Harjeevan had allowed Angela to take advantage of her, but now she was prepared—she'd never let anyone take from her again.

SILENCES

Babies crawl on a chequered blanket; a toddler holds onto a large balloon and sinks her teeth into it—*pop!* In shock, she runs into Charlotte's legs and clings to her knees. Her small face, furrowed with fright, brightens to a smile as Charlotte tousles her auburn curls. Balloons—orange, red, blue, green, pink and violet—bump together in the breeze and *Happy 60th Birthday Olivia* banners flap beneath them. Everything Charlotte has ever wanted is here at this party.

Charlotte had no idea why Father was estranged from his family. He had three sisters, three brother-in-laws (she assumed), and eleven nieces and nephews. Some of them, in turn, had children of their own. Eleven cousins and three aunts: her dream family. She knew none of them; Father never spoke about them and there were no photos of them displayed on shelves, hung on the walls or even tucked away in albums. Exclusive to their walls were posters of Father's past exhibitions—successes achieved before her birth—her own collection of competition wins, and images of her rendered in oils, pastels and watercolours.

The only member of Father's family she had contact with was Grandmother. Charlotte didn't like Grandmother, her elegance and reserve not living up to Charlotte's expectation of how a grandma ought to behave. Knitting, baking and secret treats: that was how a real grandma behaved.

Twice a year, without Father (his work kept him busy), they visited Grandmother, making the arduous trek up to London. It seemed they lived as far from her as was possible. Father would drop them off at the station (he needed the car during the day), then train, train, underground train, train again, and finally station, where Grandmother's partner, Geoff, was waiting to pick them up. Charlotte didn't like Geoff either. He had over-exuberant eyebrows and hair that protruded from his ears and nostrils. As she settled in the car, putting on her seatbelt, he grabbed her nose and exclaimed, "I've cut your rudder off!" Then he laughed, snorting through his nostrils. It was creepy.

On arrival, Charlotte was ushered into the living room and there Grandmother sat, a slender Queen Victoria, glorious upon her throne. Grandmother held out her cheek and Charlotte was expected to pay homage with a single peck. Once she was brave enough to give a facetious bow, which was met with an embarrassed slap from Mother.

Afraid to utter a sound, Charlotte picked her way across the room, avoiding glass cabinets filled with Royal Dalton chinaware ("Do be careful, darling, I've been collecting those for years ...")

and miniature classical columns on which sat vases replete with tasteful bouquets. Sitting with her knees together on the Regency-style handcrafted sofa ("Please don't spill anything, darling; dove-grey is prone to the most awful stains ..."), she watched the rotating bronze innards of the mantelpiece clock, waiting for the bell to ring, marking out every fifteen minutes. After squash was drunk and answers about schoolwork, music and competition successes were squeezed from her ("You don't want to follow in your father's footsteps ..."), often completed by Mother, they left, once again undergoing the ritual of the peck on the cheek. Grandmother never made return visits.

Aunties Veronica and Isabella chat, half-watching the children play. They sip from glasses of cool white wine. Uncles cluster, quaffing beer. Auntie Olivia leads Charlotte around the garden, introducing her to cousins: Cousin Adam owns his own landscaping business (he designs gardens for the great and good); Cousin Beth is a lecturer at the local college (she is ever so clever and knows it); Cousin Luke's an electrician (his nickname is Thor—old joke about him nearly electrocuting himself); Violet is a jewellery designer and maker (look, she made this beautiful ring as a birthday gift); Davey, a nail technician (he gives the entire family free nails); Lucia, an architect (she's passionate about sustainable housing); Sebastian, an occupational therapist (specialises in modern dance); Stuart, a film archivist (being alone in a dark room all the time makes him a little cranky); Ewan is in retail (but is really a comedian); and Amelia and Zara look after all the kids (they must have done something terrible in their past lives).

"Please, Florence, visit him; I know he misses you and would want to see you. And Charlotte would love to show you around the village. It would be good for her to have a closer relationship with her grandmother." Charlotte sat glued to her usual spot on the Regency-style sofa (with the delicate dove-grey upholstery), knees clamped together, leaning over as far as she could, straining to overhear Mother's imploring voice as they spoke in the hallway.

"You understand nothing," Grandmother retorted.

"Then explain. I want to know; it's been going on for too long." Mother sounded exasperated.

Geoff crept into the room and quietly shut the door behind him, cutting Charlotte off from the conversation. Laughing his nasal snort, he sat down beside her and put his hand under her chin.

"Get out of that without moving."

She stared at him, unimpressed.

Charlotte wasn't surprised that this was the last visit to Grandmother she made with her mother. Grandmother was so mean.

Children run criss-cross over the lawn, shouting and laughing as they reach for bubbles floating in the air. Delicate rainbows emerge into shapes and burst before they can be caught. Two children scramble to catch an enormous, bulbous bubble. A boy, slight of frame, is thrust to the ground by a much larger girl.

Unused to terraced housing, Charlotte feels uneasy at being overlooked by the buildings flanking either side of Auntie Olivia's house. The neighbours' windows are black and impenetrable—anyone could be watching.

The children aren't bothered; they dance under striped bunting, which weaves over the garden, containing them like a web. It protects them, at least a little, from unseen observers. Crying and dishevelled, the boy lies on the grass, rubbing his knees.

Grandmother Florence shouts, a baby on her hip. "Be careful. Play nicely." Grandmother stands next to her sister, Elizabeth, and the two elders giggle together like girls. Charlotte didn't know Grandmother had a sister. She watches their laughter, wishing she had a sister too.

"Do call me 'Grandma', dear. 'Grandmother' is so formal."

Charlotte is ecstatic. This is her initiation into an equal relationship with Grandma, one that her cousins have enjoyed all their lives.

Mother was gone within two weeks of the separation announcement. Adamant to stay, Charlotte had defied Mother's demands to leave with her. Mother's neediness was sad and made Charlotte furious. Father was her favourite parent. He had always taken care of her, bathing and dressing her, brushing and styling her hair, doing his best to adhere to her insistence on intricate hairstyles that came in and out of fashion. Mother never had the patience. Father was there.

Lingering at the doorway of his workshop, Charlotte inhaled, luxuriating in the smell of freshly cut wood. Watching Father as he worked was hypnotic, and the sounds of sawing and sanding drew her into his world. Creeping unnoticed across the expanse of the studio, she would try to make him jump. He was engrossed in his work and the noise of the machinery would disguise her steps—or so she thought. As she got within five paces, he would suddenly rise up, growling like a bear, and lift her, squealing, into the air. She'd wrap her legs around his torso and squeeze, clamping onto him, unwilling to go down.

After Mother left, their routine continued, unhindered, and they slipped into quiet unison. Father cooked. She cleaned. Things were easier with just the two of them.

Auntie Olivia's party is a success. Everyone welcomes Charlotte with smiles and kisses. They comment on her family resemblance. Button noses, brown eyes (ranging from amber to chocolate) and the points of chins are compared. She has the family curls, the long caramel waves reaching down her back. They ask about her A Levels (history, art and theatre studies) and her likes (country walks and the smell of wood shavings) and dislikes (cauliflower and being rushed—assignment deadlines are hell). She tells them about her ambition to go to art college just like Father, but moving away from the countryside will make her sad, she knows. Auntie Olivia invites her to stay with her if she gets some work experience in London (being with family will make it easier). No one asks after Father. The etiquette around mentioning Father is unclear ("Father helped me with my drawing competition entry …", "Father took me hiking …"). Confusion silences her, and her life with Father remains hidden.

Bang, whistle, wow! Gold and silver showers make them gasp. Cinnamon and ginger aromas fill the air. "Deck the halls with boughs of holly!", "Merry Christmas everyone!", "Three, two, one—happy New Year!", "18! Now you're an adult, how do you feel?" Still no one mentions Father. The family also remain a secret to him.

Each meeting makes her feel worse.

As if dunked into freezing water, Charlotte can't catch her breath. Father's coldness is shocking. Chilling. After almost a year, she had to tell him. Sneaking around, hiding her visits, has made her feel dirty, her pleasure siphoned away with each lie.

Then Auntie Olivia asks her to join the family on holiday. This lie is far too huge for Charlotte to keep. A hope lingers that seeing her burgeoning relationship with his family will trigger a desire in him to reunite with them. Instead, he doesn't look at her and keeps his head fixed in one position as she breaks the news of her holiday plans. Shouting and screaming was never part of her family life. Even when Mother accused Father of flirting with the women from the village (he was always a catch), he simply smirked, amused at her accusation, and then ignored it. The only way Charlotte could tell her parents were having an ongoing argument was that the doors shut with a little more force than usual. And even that rapidly diminished.

Now she understands the dynamic of her life. Father retreats, locking her out of his world. Their world. The silence is impossible to endure. It's a velvet, cosseting oppression that eradicates her existence and leaves only the sighs of summer grass and the buzzing of flies. She longs for fury, recriminations and broken objects.

She goes anyway.

From the time Mother left, Charlotte didn't see Grandmother. Nearly a year passed and Charlotte, without admitting it to herself, decided that she had no intention of visiting Grandmother again—until, that is, she formulated her plan. Then, she took the train alone, rode to Grandmother's with Geoff, and endured the usual polite conversation.

Excusing herself (the loo) she sped around the house until she found, sitting neatly on a tidy desk, a phone.

With speed, she scrolled down. Her grandmother knew an enormous number of people (Abigail, Adam, Bernard, Beth, Cecil, Celia: the names merged into a mass of letters). In her haste, she couldn't work out how to jump further down the alphabet.

"Darling, what are you doing?" Grandmother called from the sitting room.

"Looking for something in my jacket, Grandmother." The names wouldn't stop. She hadn't even made it to the Gs.

"You won't find it by tampering with my mobile phone!" Grandmother snatched the phone from Charlotte's grip. Stealth was not an attribute she'd associated with Grandmother. Humiliated, she couldn't help the quivering of her lip, which was soon followed by a trickle of tears, and then a desperate howl.

Grandmother spoke in a gentle, coaxing manner. "What were you looking for?" Tears dribbled down Charlotte's face, crawling over her lips. She couldn't answer. Grandmother pushed a tissue into her hand. "There's no need to cry, darling. I'm not angry." Grandmother maintained her new, surprising tone. Hiccupping and snorting, Charlotte attempted an answer.

"*Trying to find …*" Shuddering and choking, she tried again. "*Trying to find Auntie Olivia's number.*" The tears continued.

"*Darling, why didn't you ask?*" Grandmother gave her a peck on the forehead.

A chaos of children marches off towards the bus, eager to get to the beach. Each one disappears into the bushes until only their chattering and laughing is heard. Auntie Isabella shouts instructions above the din. "Don't go too far ahead, Thomas. Wait for the rest of us."

A second party remains at the lake house. Bare legs dangling over the end of the jetty, Charlotte's feet skim the top of the cool water. She observes the lake, a piece of charcoal poised above an empty page. Overshadowed by curvaceous willows and tall alders, the lake is enclosed. Along its shore sprout dense patches of rush and reeds, whilst white and yellow lily pads balance without breaking the tension of its surface. Light reflects on the water, shadows from the trees break it into dark fragments and sharp flashes shine into her eyes, momentarily obscuring her vision.

Sketching a moving object is difficult. Willows dip their fingertips into the water, as if these extra roots will prevent their quivering and swaying under command of the wind. Still, it's a skill she must develop, if she is to continue winning the competitions Father insists she enter (good for her career).

Today reminds her of the beautiful summer afternoons when she would walk with Father along the lane, their clasped hands swinging back and forth. Settling down at their favourite spot at the edge of their lake, they would lie together, listening to the sounds of the woods. Whilst she lounged with her arms stretched out above her head and her eyes closed, Father would sketch. In just a few strokes of the pencil he could conjure an image so like the original she would wonder if he had magic powers. He told her that if she wanted to draw she had to look. Open her eyes and observe. To create a picture is to understand an object, a motion, an emotion. Then he would draw her. She kept her own sketchbook. At first it was rough and naïve, but as she observed Father's technique, watching and replicating, her skill grew. It became a shared pleasure, a secret between the two of them. No one, not even Mother, could penetrate their world.

Charlotte listens. A wood pigeon coos, water plops as the oars of a rowboat drop into the lake, and cutlery clanks upon crockery. Her stomach rumbles, ready for lunch. Cousin Adam runs up behind her, grabs her by the shoulders and pretends to push her into the water. She squeals as he jumps into the lake.

"This isn't the time for swimming! Lunch will be ready in a minute," Auntie Olivia shouts.

This is Charlotte's ideal holiday, except Father isn't here. She misses him.

Adam climbs out of the lake and, still dripping with water, hugs Charlotte from behind. She squeals again as cold liquid seeps into her clothes.

"You're better than a towel," he laughs.

"Leave Charlotte alone and come and sit at the table." Auntie Olivia pretends to be stern. Charlotte settles into a seat next to Cousin Zara.

"Thanks for the food, Olivia. It's delicious," Zara says as she heaps a spoonful of couscous onto her plate.

"Yes, absolutely lovely. Thank you." Charlotte is keen to be grateful.

Colourful salads are dotted across the table. Chargrilled yellow and orange peppers are mixed with couscous, asparagus with green leaves are topped with the pink gems of pomegranate seeds, and a mix of heritage toma-toes, purple, red and black, are dressed with basil leaves. Three large plates of kebabs, one lamb, one chicken and one haloumi cheese, all drip with a different dressing of sticky chilli, barbecue or pesto.

"You're too kind." Auntie Olivia bows her head in fake modesty.

"Having a good time?" Cousin Zara asks Charlotte.

"The best." Charlotte beams and holds up her sketch.

"Not bad. You've captured the shadows well," Cousin Violet says.

"Ooooh—captured the shadows—hark at her!" Adam mocks, laughing.

Charlotte laughs too and replies to Violet. "You're all brilliant at what you do. I want to be as good as you and Father. He's a great furniture maker, but his artwork is even better—it's incredible." Nobody answers. She continues to fill the silence. "He's done some amazing watercolours of the lake near our house, and I modelled for one as the tragic Undine. He went through a tragic water nymphs phase." Charlotte laughs. Nobody else does. A fly lands on a piece of lamb: its feet sink into the sticky sauce. Adam swats it away.

"How do you make the dressing for the kebabs, Mum?" Lucia asks. "I think the sticky chilli is your best so far."

"If you gave us some help in the kitchen, you'd know," Grandma says.

They all begin chatting again at the same time, speaking quickly, relieved the tension has been broken. This is the first time she's talked about Father since Auntie Olivia's sixtieth. No one has mentioned him. Ever. Now that she has, everyone is awkward and silent. That's it. She has to know.

"Auntie Olivia?" Charlotte draws out her words in a sing-song fashion.

"Yes, Charlotte." Auntie Olivia mirrors Charlotte's style.

"What happened with Father? Why doesn't anyone speak about him?" Charlotte feels the atmosphere thicken with pensive silence.

"You know. Just the usual sibling rivalry." Auntie Olivia tries to sound casual.

"I'm an only child—I don't know."

The silence is volatile, dangerous. Conversations ignite and die, consuming each other.

"Siblings," begins Auntie Olivia, "siblings are … rivalry is … It's possible to love someone dearly and hate them in equal measure. Want the best for them but find it impossible to be around them." She gives Charlotte a hard smile, warming to her explanation. "It's the nature of it—"

"Answer me this." Uncle Michael interrupts. He's trying to be jovial, but she can feel his anger as he leans closer. "If a family member has, let's say, difficult political beliefs, is a racist or has done terrible things like murder or embezzled from a charity, what should be done about them?"

"Michael, leave it." Auntie Olivia clips her words but it still sounds like pleading.

The cousins look at one another.

"We'll start the washing up." Adam shoots over his shoulder as he, Violet and Luke half-run into the house.

The family has conversations and debates, even arguments, on a variety of topics, but never have any of them been this intense. A moment ago they'd been discussing food, in a beautiful setting, in the cool shade of the veranda. Now it's frightening.

"I'm not quite sure what you mean." Charlotte tries to understand the dark mood.

"I'll make it clearer," Uncle Michael persists. "Let's say you've supported someone's success, helped them achieve beyond anyone's expectations, nurtured and loved them. Should you shun them for their appalling actions? How about reporting them to the authorities and getting them sent to jail? Rehabilitated? Should everyone be told the truth so they can decide for themselves if they want to associate with this person?"

"I don't understand." Charlotte doesn't want to think about these questions. He continues.

"You're an artist. Right then, I'll put it in terms you'll understand. Eric Gill, for example. His sculptures are incredible; one even hangs over the doors of the BBC. He invented one of our most popular fonts, one people use every day. He was charismatic, charming—people wanted to be around him. But he believed in 'pushing the boundaries of his sexuality,' which in everyday talk means he had sex with his sisters and daughters. Should he have been shunned? Arrested? Or, thanks to his genius, have his actions been swept under the carpet? If he is held to account, should his work be discarded? Should the BBC rip down his sculpture and the font he invented be banned?"

"So you think we should destroy it all?" A question seems to Charlotte the best way to defuse the situation.

"Maybe. So-called 'creatives' get away with murder because they're supposedly 'geniuses'," Michael creates inverted commas with his fingers. "Even though their victims suffer lifelong trauma." His anger's no longer contained.

Charlotte wants to run. "Can't we do both—appreciate the art and punish the person?" It seems a reasonable compromise to her.

"Please, Michael, she's just a child. Stop."

Michael spins to face Olivia. "No, she's not. She's an adult now." Then he spins back to Charlotte. She closes her arms around her body, terrified by the violence that threatens. "If we do that for the artist, what do we do with the other perverts? If a policeman is an exemplary policeman but a pervert, does that mean he could still be a good police officer? Still work with the public? With children? What about doctors and nurses? Carpenters?"

Charlotte was silent; she didn't know what to do.

"I tell you what happens to them. They get sidelined, pushed out of public life, ostracised. But not artists. Why should these alleged 'creatives' have licence to do what they like?"

"Because they're special, I guess." It is wrong. She's said the wrong thing.

"Special! They're fucking perverts." He stands up. He seems enormous.

"Dad, please." Lucia also stands up.

"Yes, stop this now, Michael, it's enough. I'll deal with this later." Grandma stands in front of him to block his access to Charlotte.

"I think I'll go and help Cousin Adam in the kitchen." A fixed smile on her face, Charlotte walks with an exaggerated bounce in each of her steps. As soon as she reaches the porch, she sobs aloud and runs into the house.

Children run around the house, their steps reverberating through the wooden structure. Water runs into baths and children scream with pleasure as they wage war, splashing one another. Their chattering decreases as they are told to calm down and climb into bed. At last the house is silent. On holiday, this is the time when the day is at an end and the evening has yet to begin. Everyone disappears into secret worlds and only murmurs remain.

There's a gentle knock on the door.

"Charlotte, darling, are you awake? I've made a fresh pot of tea. Would you care to join me?" Grandma speaks through the bedroom door.

Charlotte looks in the mirror. Her eyes are puffy, red raw from crying.

"I've got some of your favourite tarts." Embarrassed by her own behaviour, Charlotte can't face the family. "Please, darling. It will only be us for tea."

Grandma is sitting alone in the front porch. Its pale wooden panels absorb light from the setting sun. Steam rises from the golden liquid as it pours from the teapot into antique china cups. Just beneath their rims sits a pert ring of tiny pink roses. A plate of tarts is piled high with a Cherry Bakewell perched on top.

"Eat up," Grandma says, just as a grandma should. Taking a large gulp of tea, she then exhales with pleasure. Light shines through her silver curls, bestowing her with a golden halo. Charlotte picks up a tart and bites into it. It's glorious — the sweet, white icing and plentiful jam stick to her teeth as she chews. "Has he ever touched you?"

Charlotte coughs pastry. "Uncle Michael? No, but he can be a bit frightening." She takes another bite, working the cherry into her mouth with her top lip.

"Your father. Has he ever interfered with you? Touched you in any way you're uncomfortable with?"

Charlotte is nauseated; the Cherry Bakwell congeals in her throat.

In the long quiet of the slumbering house, clarity emerges. Now she is awake. Now she understands why Mother suddenly left, and her pleas for Charlotte to live with her. And why Father hadn't fought the divorce settlement. Why they are alone, just the two them. And why Uncle Michael is furious. And Father's sisters: Isabella, Violet and Lucia.

But. This is Father. He's never done anything to her, only taken care of her, nurtured and inspired her.

"Your aunts and I, we did what we could. What was possible at the time. We couldn't make him face justice; it would have been impossible, the girls' word against his. I couldn't put them through that despite the demands of Uncle Michael."

Instead, they'd sent him into the dark places: no family, no old friends, no contacts from his nascent world of art. Instead, his art remained undeveloped and finally forgotten. They'd bartered his successful art career for their silence.

She had been their gamble.

"So, you've come back," is all Father says. It's been over a month since they've seen each other. Or had contact of any kind. She's missed him in every joint and muscle. Her existence is so perfectly bound with his that she couldn't conceive of life without him. Her art was weaker without his critical eye. She couldn't see clearly without him. To be the artist she wants to be, she needs him.

During the remaining interminable weeks of sunshine and nature and good food, she'd made her decision. She wouldn't lose him. She couldn't.

His face softens to a smile, perceptible to only the two of them.

Standing once more in the doorway of his workshop, Charlotte inhales the smell of wood. It makes her delirious with pleasure. She shuts her eyes and breathes in deep, holding onto its essence.

The silence is of a different nature now. Now she understands it; now she controls it.

Secrets work both ways. She's gained her family, the family she's always dreamed of. She wouldn't let them go. And she also intends to keep Father.

She would keep the family secret. And her own.

HOOKED

She was fishing. Definitely fishing. Holding out her hand, she thrust her engagement ring into my line of vision. It was magnificent: art deco, and within the trio of diamonds were trapped tiny rainbows.

I couldn't tell the truth.

"Looks expensive," was my dismal compromise. I avoided eye contact, but I'd made the mistake of mentioning the value.

"It was. I chose a cheaper solitaire, but Bryan insisted I have the more expensive trio. He's such a sweetheart." I doubted it was his choice. She smiled so smugly it made me want to twist her nose until she fell on her knees, screaming.

She'd never give a direct compliment, not to our faces. Behind our sisters' backs, I'd listen to her proclaiming, "Tara is beautiful in *all* the photographs" and "Ruth is *so* clever at her studies." She'd emphasize 'all' and 'so'. Most bizarre was her own inability to endure anything less than the kindest of words. Any comment short of a gushing review provoked either volcanic anger or hysterical crying.

It was behaviour that warned, "Keep off the grass or I'll eradicate your entire existence from the planet earth." Consequently, honesty was not a guiding principle of our relationship.

"We're renovating the entire house before the wedding," she informed me, her voice replete with pride.

So here we sat at a restaurant table, her fishing for anything she might hook to feed her insatiable emotional need and me avoiding the line. Avoiding the fact that she'd been uncomfortable with my existence from the moment of my birth, when she'd said to our exhausted mother, "What did you bring *that* home for?" She'd emphasised 'that'. Or that's how Mum tells it.

The waitress rested the edge of a black tray on the table. Maintaining perfect balance, she plucked a green glass bottle and started to pour liquid into Mary's glass. We watched as the level of the fluid rose.

"I asked for fizzy water." Raising her eyebrows and pulling her lips back into a sneer, Mary looked up at the waitress. This face was a common feature of shopping trips and dining out. I'd seen her belittle a young cashier for talking too enthusiastically to a customer ahead of us in the queue: "Must you waffle so much? Some of us have places to go. *Today*." She'd emphasised 'today'. But this waitress was gracious. Mary's rudeness didn't even seem to register. Instead, she apologised, promising to return with the correct beverage. I knew what Mary would say: "Honestly, how hard can it be?" And she did.

Considering this behaviour, I was pretty sure her

reaction to my being candid would be less than positive. It was the form it would take that intrigued me. Would she:

a) Implode with rage and melt like the Wicked Witch of the West?
b) Cry until all the moisture in her body evaporated and left her dried out like the discarded skin of a snake?
c) Smash all the glassware within her immediate vicinity, crushing them in her hands until the blood dripped from her fingers and ran down to her elbows?

I was sufficiently curious to actually toy with telling her. It would be great material. Short-term responses may have been unpredictable but the long-term consequences I was sure of. Mary was the Stalin of emotions. Anyone who crossed her suffered the same fate: they were consigned to her personal Gulag. She hadn't spoken to our parents for over twenty years, and had extended that silence to anyone who had dared to raise concerns. An array of aunts, uncles, cousins and friends were all lost to her. Once they were out of sight, they were completely out of mind and it would not be too harsh to say that, for her, they never existed. In our teens, Mary and I once spent eight months locked in complete silence. If something urgently needed to be communicated, we'd talk across the bedroom via our two younger sisters. I can't recall the exact cause of the quarrel but, like an aircraft accident, it's never a single element that leads to disaster. The situation was resolved when Mum finally reached snapping point. Neither of us could misunderstand her exacerbation and we started to talk as if the eight months were eight minutes. When the incident of this row cropped up in conversation years later, Mary referred to it as "when you went odd".

So I came up with a wiser strategy, a third way: to not tell her the truth—but also not to lie.

Third Way Examples

Lie: "Yes, I can see you've lost weight, your face is much thinner."

Truth: "No, of course you haven't lost any weight and, by the way, I found all those empty crisp packets under the sofa."

Compromise: "It's hard to lose weight—keep at it."

Lie: "That wallpaper is just perfect for your spare room."

Truth: "I couldn't care less about how you decorate your spare room. Why are you bothering, anyway? The room is spare!"

Compromise: "Decorating again? How do you find the energy?"

Lie: "I know. Finding his unwashed breakfast bowl in the sink every morning must be unbearable."

Truth: "Really. Is that all you've got to worry about in a relationship? Sister, you are seriously spoiled."

Compromise: "I suppose it takes time to get used to someone else's habits."

Tara rushed up to the table. "So sorry I'm late." She sat down and unwound her gingham scarf.

"Always the glamorous and late one." Mary nodded to Tara as she removed her jacket to show an elegant mustard shirt that contrasted with her scarlet lips. Her outfit must have cost three months of my income. Tara gave a nervous titter. She bent across to hug me and I clasped at her birdlike frame. I hoped the conversation would be easier now we were three.

"Is Ruth coming?" Tara enquired, as she settled into her seat.

"No. You know how unreliable she is." Mary again delivered her definitive judgment.

"She's got exams." I dared to balance the scales. As a family, we usually met every few months. A twisted complicity of 'we're all in it together' left us like limpets clinging to a rock as life crashed on our heads. An outsider could never understand our shared history; we were addicted to one another. Or perhaps to our dysfunctionality. I find it hard to separate the two.

Today's impromptu meeting, I now understood, was to announce the engagement. Brothers need not apply; they would be less than impressed by her trio of diamonds.

Tara picked up the menu and scanned the list of dishes. "Have you ordered?"

"Not yet …" I started to offer an explanation but Mary interjected.

"We didn't get a chance. The waitress got our drinks order wrong and we're still waiting for her. It seems she's gone to the source of the spring to retrieve it."

"I'm sure she'll be here in a minute. Gives me time to choose." Tara tittered again and went back to perusing the menu. Mary's eyes followed as a waiter passed, holding two overflowing plates of food. On one sat a burger, piled high with browned onions and cheese moulded to the meat. She sucked at her teeth, swallowing excess saliva.

"That looks great, doesn't it, Mary?" Tara exchanged her titter for a loud, full laugh as her eyes also followed the food.

"How do you stay so skinny?" Mary asked in a petulant tone. "I normally like what you wear, but those trousers could do with an extra inch." Tara was now Mary's target.

"Skinny-tight is all the style. Not that you concern yourself with that." Tara tried to keep her smile but withered at yet another conflict. "I could help you with an exercise regime, if you'd care to join me at the gym."

Tears like diamonds shone in the corner of Mary's eyes. But, true to form, she hit back. "I'll leave the skeletons for Halloween, thanks very much." She spat her retort across the table, as a solitary tear hit the white tablecloth.

Ha! I was glad Tara had said it. Mary was desperate to be slim again but was unprepared to put in the work. Exercise of any kind bored her. She would give up after only a few minutes, collapsing and panting like a crashed airman crawling across the desert in search of water: unable to endure the searing heat, he cries out in desperation, half mad, "I can't go on!" I wished I could shake her, slap her face and demand she pull herself together.

Her fiancé was the only person I'd seen able to get Mary to act in a reasonable fashion. During a cycling trip—cycling being a favoured family activity—the wind had been particularly harsh, which made the ride hard going. Mary had struggled on, becoming slower and increasingly angry at each push on the pedal, until she'd dropped her bike in the middle of the road and collapsed, crying with frustration and exhaustion. As usual, we'd all ignored her and continued on. But Bryan had stopped, turned around and cycled back to her, picked her up off the road and within a few moments she was back on the bike. He'd ridden behind her, shouting, "Come on! Not much further now." And it had worked. She'd calmly ended the ride with a smile on her face. We were amazed. It was a miracle none of us could ever have performed. From then on, Bryan was nicknamed 'The Saint'. What he sees in her is unfathomable, but then love is blind. And in Bryan's case, also deaf and mute.

As the waitress approached, Mary smiled, the tears long since dried.

"At last. Were you carbonating the water yourself?" Mary raised one eyebrow at the waitress. I closed my eyes in a bid to absent myself.

"Would you like to order?" The waitress completed her task and lightly drew her hands together, holding them in front of her.

"Yes, ten minutes ag—"

"I'll have the rocket salad, thanks," Tara cut in.

"Is that all? I'm surprised you don't conk out lifting a fork—you peck like a sparrow."

Tara nodded towards Mary's stomach. "You don't." She burst into a loud laugh.

The waitress looked in my direction and we both battled to suppress our smiles. The waitress was handling Mary well. Mary switched her attention.

"Aren't you going to write it down?" she demanded.

"I'll remember." The waitress smiled, turning to look at me. But Mary couldn't stop.

"Well, you got the drinks wrong." We both ignored her.

"The fishcakes, please. Thank you so much." I smiled hard and wide, making sure she knew I didn't hold the same resentment against her as Mary did. She turned back to Mary with a fixed grin.

"And for you, ma'am?" Mary was leaning over, her snout sticking into the menu. Without looking up, she said, "Double cheeseburger, well done, with bacon and extra fries. Can you remember all—"

"Very good," the waitress said, beating her retreat. Dieting may be the priority for most blushing brides-to-be, but not for Mary. I found it hard to believe Bryan still fancied her, but then he was a saint.

"Err, aaawkwaard." Tara sang the word to lessen her embarrassment.

"The woman's obviously an idiot."

I cringed. Mary was eternally ungrateful, nothing satisfied her. It was exhausting, but she would never realise it; she saw it as her right to demand what she wanted and to say what she thought, despite the consequences and how it might make others feel.

"Anyway, if you're going to keep being so mean, I won't ask you to be my bridesmaid." She held out her hand for Tara to admire her engagement ring. Tara smiled.

"Congratulations! It's beautiful, and I'd love to be bridesmaid." Typical Tara, always keen to dress up. I watched her lean over and kiss Mary. A traitor's kiss.

"And you, if you want to." She looked at me and

continued without waiting for my reply. "I'll buy the shoes and accessories, but you'll have to pay for your own dresses." She flopped open a bridal magazine and pointed to a simple but elegant empire-line dress.

"This is the one I want—they're only six hundred each." She was glowing with excitement.

"Couldn't we get them made much cheaper? It looks pretty simple." Sixty pounds stretches my budget, six hundred would be a miracle.

"It's not that bad and it *is* a special occasion. Sales a bit thin at the moment?" Tara asked.

"Oh, you know what it's like this time of the year, getting ready for the exhibition, and then there's the rent on the studio." I dreaded any talk about money: now I'd get the parental lecture.

"You should get a proper job, with a proper income." What Mary meant was a proper job like hers, in finance, and not faffing around with tissue paper and string, as she thought of my sculptures. Although the compliment wasn't returned, I admired her; she'd started as a bank clerk and worked her way up to broker. Mary continued, "Schools need good teachers, even in the arts. And don't roll your eyes—you know I'm right." Teaching was her solution for my precarious 'arty' lifestyle.

"Do you think you'll make it along to the exhibition?" I said, as a diversion as much as a genuine question.

"Defo. But no freebies—I'll pay for my tickets." Tara was enthusiastic about my work, but I knew what Mary would say.

"I'll try, but I'm so busy with work, the house renovations

and now the wedding." She never came to any of my exhibitions.

"Have you got enough money to keep you going? I could lend or give you some, if you need it." Tara opened her Gucci purse.

"No, please, no need. It's not too bad, if I'm careful." I'd rather do without than be obligated to any family member again. It was too humiliating.

Mary was enjoying the show; she part-laughed, part-scolded. "And we know how bad you are at that. Money has always slipped through your fingers like sand."

"Well, it's—" I began, only to be interrupted.

"Do you remember that time when you were nine and spent all your holiday money on the first day, and cried until Mother felt sorry for you and gave you some more?" She scoffed, content in her self-righteous analysis. "You always knew how to con Mother and she was fool enough to fall for it."

I felt as if I'd been thrown from an aeroplane over enemy territory. My stomach plummeting to the ground, I spoke the truth. "That's not how it was, not at all." I refused to be the dependent, financially imbecilic younger sister just to keep the peace. I continued. "I lost my purse and it was Nan who replaced the money, not Mum." Uncompromising. I had abandoned the third way.

"Doesn't change the fact, you're still irresp—"

But it was my turn to interrupt.

"If you had bothered to notice what was really going on instead of being so corrupted by an insatiable need for constant attention, you might be less bitter. You don't listen to or care about anyone else. It's always about you and if it isn't, you can't stand it. Even as I kid I could see how hard Mum worked to keep you happy and how difficult you made it for her, for all of us, and I just wanted to make it a bit easier."

I was standing. Mary stared at me, silent. Tara held her hand over her mouth to hide her smirk. The blood still drained from my head, I dropped into my seat. What was she going to do? I couldn't stand the silence. Would her reaction be a, b or c? Then she spoke.

"Not think about others? That's all I did. That's all I was permitted to do. Have you ever thought how hard it was for me? Paul and I were fine as a duo but then you came along. Then Graham, then Tara, and finally Ruth. All cuter, happier, cleverer or funnier. When Mother had her breakdown and Father fucked off God knows where every night, I suddenly became just the eldest girl, forced to look after you all, dress you, feed you, applaud your little triumphs, while Paul spent all his time on Nintendo—and everybody thought that was normal. I wanted to go to university, to travel and do all the usual things teenagers do, but I couldn't because I had to look after you fucking ungrateful lot. And I didn't go into banking for my health, but to pay the rent and put food in your mouths. And not a word of thanks from any one of you."

I was astonished. No shouting, broken glass or meltdown, no a, b or c. Instead, bitterness delivered with quiet acrimony; her venom saturating and painful. This was an outcome I couldn't have ever envisioned: an option d.

I now understood we'd all been struggling with our own

family fallout. I'd assumed we weren't just all in it together but we were all fighting the same battle. I was wrong.

Our plates were dropped in front of us.

"Looks delicious. Thank you." Tara looked up at the waitress.

"Yes, lovely, thank you," Mary agreed. "Yours looks fantastic." Mary pointed at my fishcakes with her fork.

"Really good." Even if they looked awful, I would have said they were the best fishcakes I'd ever seen. And apparently so would Mary.

"If you ring her today she'll give you one last chance. She'll still even let you be a bridesmaid," Tara said. It was four months since Mary and I had spoken.

"And you didn't tell her, did you?" I asked.

"I do value my life!" Tara laughed. Ruth's birthday had passed without celebration, it being too problematic to organise the warring factions. The wedding date had been set and preparations were going ahead.

My exhibition, *War and Peace: the Art of Sibling Rivalry*, had been a success. Without knowing it, Mary had been the star of the show. Our relationship was laid bare in all its complexity. If it hadn't been for Mary, no one would have read to me as a child or let me sleep in their bed when I was afraid. If it hadn't been for Mary, no one would have given me a home when I couldn't pay my rent or topped up my bank account when I'd gone overdrawn.

The reviews were good and exhibition-goers complimented me on how well the forensic reconstructions of family life captured the essence of sibling rivalry. They reassured me that they too had these kinds of love/hate relationships. For the first time ever, I made money from an exhibition. It seemed to have raised my profile, and I was invited to show at more prestigious events.

"So, you've decided to stop acting crazy. I'm not sure what that was all about." I listened to Mary's voice and imagined her camel-like sneer. She'd landed me, hook, line and sinker. And yet, I'd also landed her.

"Indeed." I forced a laugh and quickly continued. "What have you been up to?"

"Oh, you know, the wedding arrangements. You're just in time—I was about to order the dresses. Size 6 for Tara, you and Ruth size 8, is that right?" She didn't wait for my answer. "And can you believe I'm still a 10? I shouldn't have eaten that burger," she laughed, "but that's what happens when you fall off the dieting wagon! And you didn't even try to stop me. It's a good thing Bryan keeps me on track or, God forbid, I'd be a size 12, especially around you three Skinny Minnies."

Baby elephant, golden goose and poisonous scorpion: this was the relationship that just kept giving.

"And finally! We've managed getting around to having the kitchen done. I've gone for green. You'll have to come round and let me know what you think of the tiles."

IMMERSION

I t isn't a dream, she can hear it. Singing, all around, saturating, indistinguishable from the running of water, echoing …

Set adrift on lonely oceans
Hard I tried to keep my smile …

"Pop the immersion on please, Tess," Mum says. With her thumb and forefinger Tess pushes hard until the switch clicks to reveal its red topside. An intense whoosh gives way to rumbling, the sound reverberates, and the immersion heater sings out its deep, soothing melody. The Sunday night ritual begins.

First, it's her turn. Using the bath as a slide, Tess plunges into the bubbles. Luxuriating in their silken froth, she turns over on her front; now a mermaid, her legs become a fishtail and she flicks it between the bubbles and the water. Rolling over again, she lies, immersed, under the water, her long hair seaweed, tangled within itself.

Later, when she is dry and in her pyjamas, she sits cross-legged, eating buttered crumpets in front of the television. She watches images of countries that she had no idea existed and makes a pact with herself: one day she'll explore the earth's mysteries for herself.

On the ward Tess isn't allowed baths. Everything is supervised. She showers under scrutiny, eats under scrutiny and sleeps under scrutiny. But they don't know that everything will be alright when her mum comes to take her home. Mum will tell them she is well; she isn't a danger to anyone, least of all herself.

The art therapist, Sophie—still a young woman herself, with long beads caught in her voluminous hair—asks Tess what brings her comfort. The baths, the ritual, the safe sounds of Sunday evenings, she explains to Sophie, when she watches TV whilst her mum stands behind her ironing. The squeak of the ironing board, the fresh smell of clean washing and the sharp hiss of the spray-starch tells her everything is okay, everything is calm. Martha, the new baby, sleeps in her Moses basket. Tess thinks her head smells of milk, peaches and sunny days on the beach.

Tess can never understand why she can't stay at home with Mum and the baby. It's baffling. Every day Mum walks her to school, pushing Martha in her buggy with Tess hanging onto its handlebar. Her gloved hand will sometimes slip and she'll trot to regain her position next to mum. Seeing her white breath is a novelty. She crunches on the frosted grass as her boots leave beautifully precise footprints. But each step away from home and nearer to school saps her pleasure until she becomes silent, sick at the thought of being left alone in the playground. No one has explained why school is so important. Sitting amongst a bunch of other kids just seems pointless to Tess.

It isn't gloomy and rundown like other places she's stayed. The paint is fresh and doesn't peel away from the walls, and spiders are robbed of the chance to weave their webs. This is her favourite room. An entire wall is covered with a woodland scene and she steps into the picture and walks through the spring flowers, lost amongst the trees. It's alive; in every direction wood creaks and birds sing. The doctor interrupts her daydream.

"We're very happy with your progress, Tess."

"Oh. Good. Er, thank you."

"Sophie tells us good things about your art therapy and your willingness to engage." He sits on the chair opposite, his legs crossed and hands neatly folded on his knee. Every time he switches his hands over, it catches her attention. His nails are well manicured and she wonders if he attends to them himself. "I feel confident we can relax your supervision and put you on the normal cycle throughout the night." This still means hourly checks and a full search of her bedding and room before bedtime.

Having someone watch over her whilst she is sleeping is both creepy and reassuring. She's always been afraid when alone at night, but sometimes, if she wakes up and sees the figure sitting at the end of her bed, it terrifies her: the night light's shadows on the watcher's face create a ghoulish creature, come to claim her. When she screams, a gentle voice tells her everything is okay. In those moments, her mum is speaking to her, doing her job as the keeper of her safety.

"We'll leave your medication as it is now and review it at your next meeting. Does that work for you?" He waits for her reply. The medication makes her feel less herself—the sharp vigilance of her anxiety is dulled—but there is no point arguing. The doctors ask your opinion but rarely change their minds. She nods in affirmation; it only makes it worse if she resists. Tess knows when to nod, to smile when required and she always takes her drugs. If she doesn't do what they want, or is not at least seen to do what they want, she'll never get to go home.

"I love the way you've broken this down into a house layout. Each room tells a story."

"Yes, you see, that's me in my bedroom, in bed. I'm scared of the dark." Tess points at a nest of dark hair peeping out of the top of the bedclothes. "And look, that's my mum in the bathroom, having a bath. It's nice, she's there next to my bedroom."

"Why is that important?"

"Because I can still hear her and we're all safe." Normal, safe and calm. After she's put to bed in her cosy pyjamas, chatting away to her mum, sharing her ambitious plans for world travel, she is left alone. The door is never fully closed, leaving a slice of light from the landing to fall across her bed, and as she lies awake in the semi-darkness, she listens for sounds of life. If there aren't any raised voices, she'll relax and soon hear a creak at the top of the stairs, followed by a click and ping as the bathroom light is pulled on. Next, the squeak of taps being turned on and the harsh pounding of water as it flows into the bathtub. Pipes knock overhead, and the low shush and vibration of the water tank grows large in the empty expanse of the loft. Her mum always sings as she steps into the bath. Tess hears the occasional splash of water as her mum washes each part of her body, probably with a sponge heavy with soap. Whilst the sounds of Sunday night continue, Tess knows all is well.

In the drowsy moments before sleep, she can hear it. It isn't a dream. Her mum's voice, singing, all around, saturating, indistinguishable from the running of water, echoing ...

Set adrift on lonely oceans
Hard I tried to keep my smile
On the air your singing, floating,
Lures me gently to your side ...

Water pounds, gushing from the taps, deepening in tone as the water rises, muffled by the growing mass of foam. A light flashes across the room and settles on her face. It hurts her eyes and she burrows beneath the bedclothes.

"Come on Tess, you know the rules. You can't cover your head, we need to be able to see you." The healthcare assistant pulls the sheet from her face leaving her to screw her eyes shut.

"Sorry, it's just the lights," she explains, squirming to avoid the beam of the torch.

"Okay then, try and sleep now. I'll be back later to check on you," he says as he withdraws from the room. Closing her eyes, she hears a trickle of water, developing into a rush, and her mum's voice, singing. She is safe.

"You might be able to go home for the weekend. I've spoken with Martha and she agrees." Tess knows she mustn't tell them about her mum. Whenever she speaks about her mum coming to bring her home, it makes them upset.

"Do you think that's something we can agree to work towards?" Tess nods and he returns her answer with a smile.

"I also wanted to talk to you about what happened last week with the concealed knife. I realise it's been unsettling for a lot of the residents and I wanted to check in with you about it." Tess wonders why Dr. Anand would ever be worried about her because of another patient's suicide attempt.

"I'm okay, really." Tess keeps herself apart from the other patients and is never drawn into their misdemeanours. You have to be cleverer than that. It's curious to Tess that some of her fellow inmates have meltdowns, throwing their food or spitting at the HCAs. Some even have bandages on their arms, which remain in full sight—where everyone can see! Tess thinks they are very silly to carelessly display their horrible thoughts and give away the contents of their minds. How do they ever think they'll get out with that kind of behaviour? Although, she does admire the way a blade can be hidden within a pen.

She always picks the same book from the shelf. The pictures are exquisite.

"This is my favourite." Tess shows Sophie a large double-page image of a young woman lying in a pond of water.

"What do you like about it?" Sophie asks her.

"The woman is beautiful and it's peaceful. I like the greenery and flowers; the colours are lovely. It reminds me of having a bath with my hair floating around like seaweed."

"That's a romantic way to look at it. Do you know the play *Hamlet*? And Ophelia's story in it?" Tess shakes her head. "Okay. So, when Hamlet's dad is murdered, he becomes depressed and questions life's purpose. Ophelia is abandoned by Hamlet, her potential husband, and when he accidentally kills her dad it sends her mad. Whilst collecting flowers, she falls in the river and drowns. All the flowers are symbolic of a particular aspect of her situation. The roses, youth and beauty; the violets around her neck, chastity, and death in the young; and the weeping willow, jilted love."

"That's sad. Is all love unhappy?"

"*Hamlet* is an extreme portrayal. But I don't think that all loving relationships are unhappy. What do you think?"

"Yes, I guess, maybe." Relationships confuse Tess and talking about them feels like taking an exam she can never pass.

"Can you think of a good relationship?" Tess folds her arms and slumps back in her chair. "Nobody? It doesn't necessarily have to be romantic love," Sophie prompts as she bundles her hair into a thick rope and pulls it over her shoulder to rest on one side of her neck.

"I love my sister."

"Martha? Good. Anyone else?"

"I guess my Nanna and Granddad have been together since they were twelve or something, and they seem happy enough."

"There you go. There are examples everywhere of posi-tive stories. Maybe you could try thinking of some others and perhaps add some symbolism into your artwork to clarify what you're trying to portray?"

"Are there flowers for lonely mums and their lonely children?" Tess is picking at the edge of the page.

"I don't know. I suspect there are quite a few because, without a doubt, we're all lonely at some point in life."

Martha wrestles Tess's bag from her shoulder and packs it into the boot of the car. She slams the door shut.

"Hop in! Let's get on the road." Tess revels in Martha's enthusiasm. She is enthusiastic about almost everything. Tess has always loved her. The usual rules of sibling rivalry don't apply.

"Don't forget your seatbelt—safety first," Martha recites as she turns on the ignition and continues, "Nan and Granddad are at home and they're well excited to see you. Nan baked some of her infamous rock cakes, just for you, madam." Looking over each shoulder in quick succession, Martha backs out of the parking space.

"And I'm just as excited to get you home." She puts her foot on the accelerator and drives. "Sorry to say, I've got to pop into work tomorrow morning, but you'll be in good hands. Nan and Granddad are staying tonight, so you won't be lonely."

"You don't have to worry about me. I don't need a babysitter." For a moment, Martha scrutinises her sister. The moment stretches. "Stop!" Tess half shouts, half laughs. "It's okay. I'm okay. Honestly. They wouldn't have let me out if they were worried."

"Are you sure? Nothing can happen, not on my watch."

"Yes, sir!" Tess gives an exaggerated salute.

Tess knows these roads well and can easily draw a map of the route from the hospital to home. In the same way she remembers tracing the route from school to home, longing for Mum and Martha to come and collect her. When she first starts school, she can't tell the time but the day's routine soon becomes familiar: assembly, sums, playtime, writing practice, lunchtime, nature and then arts and crafts. During arts and crafts, the teacher gives warnings of what they need to do before home time. It sets her on edge and makes her tingle with nerves. What if she doesn't get it done in time? Then what happens?

By the time Martha starts reception, things have changed. An unease has crept into the house. At night, Tess listens to the angry shouts. The ritual of bath night is drowned out by these new sounds. During long, tiring weekends, Dad sits without moving all day, silent, a dark presence that permeates the ceiling and walls. Before, he would play with Martha or listen when Tess read to him, but now he just stares into the distance. Mum offers mugs of tea and suggests family walks. He doesn't respond.

"Look, there's me in bed and Mum in the bathroom. Can you see the flowers I've added? They're symbolic. Sophie said it helps to tell a story if you use symbolism." Tess is pointing to each item as she explains her picture. "Violets symbolise death in the young."

Nan beckons Granddad and Martha into the kitchen. "I don't think she's well enough, we should take her back."

Tess listens to their voices disguised as whispers.

"Nanna, I want her home." Martha's tone abandons its usual jollity, but gives way to pleading as she adds, "And it's only a long weekend."

"I'm not sure we can cope when you're at work tomorrow."

"You make it sound like she's a rabid beast," Martha retorts.

"I can hear you, you know," Tess shouts from the living room. She didn't realise even her artwork would causesuch a fuss. "It's only a picture, Nanna." In single file they re-enter the living room and Nan sits down next to Tess.

"I know, my love, but we just want what's best for you."

Tess kisses her cheek. "It's okay, Nanna, it doesn't mean anything."

After Dad goes, Mum is often short-tempered and tense. Sometimes Dad comes to the school gates and follows behind as they walk home. He is crying, begging, telling them how much he loves them and making promises about what he'll do if he can come back home. Mum ignores him as she drags the girls behind her. Neither Tess nor Martha know if they're allowed to talk to their dad or not.

At night, when they are supposed to be in bed, they watch him from their bedroom window. Why he sits in his car, parked opposite the house, they don't know. And for hours! Eventually, flashing blue lights fill their room as the police arrive. After they hold a short conversation with their dad, he drives away.

"You're okay, aren't you Tess?" They're snuggled together in Martha's bed, just like they did as children.

"With you to look after me," Tess reassures her sister and smooths down her unruly hair. "Remember when I used to bring you home from school and it would take absolutely ages," Tess continues, laughing.

"We'd start on the Grey Lane, spend some time in the phone box and then go to the Pitt Park," Martha says, propping her head on the crook of her elbow. "And we tried to run across the chasm of death."

Tess mirrors Martha's position and says, "We'd have to run really fast to do it and not slip down into the nettles, and on the roundabout, you'd get really panicky when I pushed it too fast." What Tess never confesses to Martha is that she took these detours because she was afraid to go home. Afraid of what she'd find—terrified to leave home in the mornings and terrified to go home in the afternoons.

Drowsy at the edge of sleep, she can hear it. Her mum's voice, singing, all around, saturating, indistinguishable from the running of water, echoing …

Set adrift on lonely oceans
Hard I tried to keep my smile
On the air your singing, floating,
Lures me gently to your side …

Water pounds, gushing from the tap, deepening in tone as the water rises, muffled by the growing mass of foam. Splashing, cleansing becomes choking. Violent slapping, skin on water, frenzied struggling, gasping dies away into exhausted silence. She opens the bedroom door; Martha loiters behind her. At first the light hurts her eyes and she can only see the silhouette of her dad. But they can hear him crying, sense his panic. He lurches forward and grasps Tess by the tops of her arms.

"I'm sorry. I'm sorry, I'm so sorry." Collecting both of the girls together, he clutches them tightly. They remain stiff in his arms, scared of what he is sorry for. "I'm sorry, I didn't mean …" He trails off, weeping.

She can hear it. Her mum's voice, singing, all around, saturating, indistinguishable from the running of water, echoing. She locks the bathroom door. Water pounds, gushing from the tap, the singing continues, her mum is singing only for her …

Set adrift on lonely oceans
Hard I tried to keep my smile
On the air your singing, floating,
Lures me gently to your side
I heard you sing

Sail to shore
Sail to shore …

Deepening in tone, the water rises, muffled by the growing body of foam. She steps into the bath and immerses her body in the water.

Tender is my grace,
Come to me
Come to me …
I'm awaiting your embrace …

As she slips beneath the waterline, listening, her grand-dad bangs on the door in rhythm with the pipes; muffled shouts, strange and uncanny, far away, accompany her mum's lullaby. She feels hands tug at her seaweed hair, pulling gently, keeping her, immersed, under the water. Safe and sound, she has come home.

A LOVE STORY

Without looking, she knows he isn't there. His absence is tangible. At one time he was always there—even if twelve metres behind. His adoration had the effect of forcing her into making more of an effort: hair, clothes, makeup. Flourishing under his gaze, wanting to impress with her knowledge of London, she'd led him to tourist attractions, places she hadn't visited since childhood, hoping he'd enjoy the outings as much as she did. Lately, though, she's noticed he keeps slipping away. At first, it was for just a few minutes, but later hours, or even days. She frets. She can only think that he must be having a break, maybe for a little think, some time to himself—because who, on occasion, doesn't need some time to themselves in a relationship?

Sitting at her dining room table, Eva picks up her fork and plunges it into a bowl of noodles. Winding them around the prongs, they slither, evading capture. Lifting

of the street the couple embrace, their kiss passionate. As they wave goodbye, he looks back over his shoulder. His eyeline switches and recognition contorts his features. He's seen her. She spins on her heel and marches in the opposite direction, pretending they're strangers.

Then she doubles back.

The girlfriend returns home. She lives in a trendy area east of the centre. Eva contemplates the shift work that this woman might have: waitress, nurse, tube driver. These, somehow, do not fit; the woman's elegance suggests performance or art. Her choice of accommodation is sophisticated. The block is moderately sized and Eva cannot tell in which of the flats the woman lives, but at least she now knows the location. It is nearly eleven o'clock; this has taken much longer than she anticipated. She must go to work.

Caution is more important now that he's seen her. But following is a skill that is becoming familiar and she is prepared. In her bag she carries a flask of coffee and a packed lunch. She anticipates a long day out. A little before twelve, they leave the house. Again, they kiss and laugh as they mooch along the road. Their hands, intertwined, swing with each step. Holding back, she watches as they turn into the next road. She runs to catch up and checks around the corner. Again she runs to the next corner. In this almost comical fashion, all three arrive at the park. The couple settle in a cosy spot, enclosed by bushes: the place Eva once sat with him. Rolling on the grass, the woman lounges across him. They wrestle and she ends

up astride him, pinning his wrists to the ground. It was
for a date to this park that Eva first stood him up. He'd
kept ringing, but she'd ignored his calls—then watched
as her phone displayed his name again and again. It was
the sweetest of pleasures. Within an hour, he'd arrived at
her house, flushed and concerned. He'd explained how
worried he'd been, that he'd feared something terrible had
happened to her. Yawning, Eva had convinced him she'd
fallen asleep and had no idea of the time. Apologising,
she'd promised to make it up to him that evening.

This was the first of many broken engagements. Working
late was too obvious, so she'd add detail: her boss needed
support at a last minute out-of-hours meeting, a colleague
was desperate for her advice to complete an important
report and, her favourite, she was called upon to admin-
ister first aid to a sick colleague and then had to wait for
an ambulance. When she'd fail to give explanations, he'd
wait for her outside her workplace. Watching him from her
fifth-floor window—looking anxious and pacing, unable
to keep still—Eva had to lean against a wall for support,
fearing she might pass out from the ecstasy. She'd save
his pleading messages and listen to them over and over
again at her leisure, endorphins flooding her. This was
love, love as she'd always dreamed it would be.

He'd be present when she went home, when she ate her
meals and when she went to bed. If she met her friend, he'd
be there. Her friend would comment on his creepiness.
Eva would agree: it was awful, downright weird, but the
most terrifying thing, she'd explain to her friend, was
imagining what other twisted behaviour he was capable

of. And her heart would beat faster. She'd press her friend's hand to her breast. "Feel my heart pound," Eva would say.

Managing their physical contact with precision, she'd give him just enough to titillate, but never the satisfaction of intercourse. He'd beg for explanations. She'd tell him he was too intense, too demanding. Then, for a moment, she'd relent and allow him to hold her. She'd luxuriate, love-soaked. He'd relax too, with relief and gratitude. Then, pulling away, she'd tell him it was over, demand he leave, blame him for pushing her. A few days later, she'd relent and they'd be back together. The times apart grew longer until, finally, engaged separation became their relationship.

It had been the perfect relationship: she'd had his adoration without the messiness of sex or inconvenience of changes to her life.

Eva had been diligent about documenting his stalking from the beginning, as attentive to it as he was to her. She'd enjoyed recording the dates and times, cataloguing her journeys. She'd even drawn maps. Often, in the evenings, she'd look over her entries, planning where next to take him.

She observes the couple, lazing in the sun and is delighted when she overhears him cooing and whispering, repeating the woman's name—Lily. They look happy. But three is a crowd.

He drags her up from the ground. Eva drops the plastic mug she is holding as he tightens his grip on her clothes, twisting them into her throat. She chokes as the pressure restricts her breathing. He forces her against a car. The attack is a shock; she hadn't noticed his approach, distracted by her cup of coffee whilst she waited for his bedroom light to go out. Lily isn't staying with him; he'd never use violence otherwise.

He screams that she should leave him and his girlfriend alone, he'll call the police, she's a fucking nutter. Eva was right: his strength is incredible and it turns her on as he grinds her harder against the car. She laughs through her constricted throat. Confused by her reaction, he releases her and she hits the pavement hard. As he withdraws he threatens to kill her if he catches her again. Eva's heart is wild within her chest; she wishes her friend could be here to feel it.

It has taken nearly two weeks to understand Lily's routine. Eva has discovered Lily is a dancer and her hours are erratic. Rehearsals can take place at various times of the day and she does not return home at any set time. Eva has used her holiday allowance to make sense of this woman's life. It has not been a waste.

Now, watching Lily purchase her coffee, Eva waits for her to sit down. Taking a deep breath, she attempts to soothe her nerves. Introducing herself, Eva is polite and apologetic, reassuring Lily she does not want to alarm her or cause any upset. It's rewarding, exciting, to see Lily's face struggling with confusion and fear as Eva explains that her new partner is unstable. She never had any idea, he's always so kind to her. They always are—in the beginning, Eva tells her.

Eva also explains to Lily about the restraining order. He's not allowed to go anywhere near Eva's workplace or home or he'll be arrested and charged. The diary was an immense help: if only everyone could be as organised, the police told her. She shows it to Lily; Eva warns her to buy a diary immediately.

Her new friend is devastated. She feels betrayed and foolish that she hadn't realised that he was a wolf in sheep's clothing. She didn't know anything about the restraining order. It seemed such a promising relationship, with such a lovely guy. Eva commiserates. She'd felt the same when they'd first met; he'd acted the part of a perfect gentleman. It's not the women's fault. He's betrayed them both. They must move forward and at least they now have one another. Eva shares some advice she was given years ago: whilst you insist on staying in a dysfunctional relationship, it will stop you from being in a healthy one.

ALL TOGETHER NOW

Crowds of tourists pushed past one another, dodging the stationary trio on all sides. Some ignored them, going on their way, but mostly they glanced sidelong or occasionally stared. The family stood directly in front of the Odeon cinema at Leicester Square. A huge Spiderman crawled up its façade.

"This is so bloody typical of you." He poked her chest with a single fleshy finger. "Didn't I tell you to be careful? But you never listen to me. I wanted to take my son to see a film on an extra-large screen — and now I can't because of you." His face, red and distorted, was a few centimetres from her own.

"You wanted to give your son a memorable experience, did you? So only you're allowed to show him the good things, whilst I have to take care of the crap stuff. You could have looked after the money yourself. It wasn't my fault—I didn't plan for the purse to get stolen," she wept.

"You didn't plan to be stupid either, but it happened. The only thing we can do now is to go home."

"Do you think that I want to go home with you now? I don't want you anywhere near me. And we thought a day out would bring us closer together! I want to get as far away from you as possible."

The boy stood under the umbrella of their bodies. With clenched fists he prevented the tears from rolling down his face.

The couple's arguing was loud, audible above the crowd's din. She smiled at the boy, but he didn't respond. Attempting to read her letter as she weaved through the mass of people, she checked the time of her interview: 1:45. She looked at her watch again. It was 12:52. Someone knocked into her shoulder and she fell. Landing square on her knees, her hands outstretched, she remained still, closing her eyes.

Only the boy watched her as she rolled onto her back. People moved past, going on their way. He looked up to his mother and father; they continued their fight. The young woman got up onto one knee and then another. She rubbed the grit away and straightened her clothing.

"Are you okay?" the boy asked, reaching out a hand to help her.

She looked up and smiled. "Yes, thanks. I'll live." She opened a packet of tissues and offered one to the boy. He cleaned his face and she dabbed the blood on her grazed hands. "Now we'll both live." And she gave him a wink.

"What the hell are you doing?" the boy's father yelled. "Let's go." He yanked at his son's hand, but before he disappeared into the throng, the boy turned back and waved. The woman returned the gesture and watched as the boy merged into the crowd.

"Do you need a moment to compose yourself?"

Her hair was sticking to her forehead and she was a little out of breath. Blood seeped from a wound on her hand and she blotted it away. Offering her a glass of water, he smiled. "Happy to begin?"

She nodded. The three interviewers all settled in their chairs and stared at her. The same middle-aged man led with the first question.

"Why do you want this position in Communities and Local Government?"

Pulling at her sleeve, she faltered. "Because …"

"It's okay," he said, "take a moment."

She inhaled and closed her eyes. "I'd like to work to bring communities closer together." She stopped. The man smiled and nodded. Half smiling back at him, she continued. "Even though, in the current climate, it sometimes seems an impossible task, I think people really want change."

He thought for a moment and then made some notes. Briefly inspecting a document, the thin woman observed her.

"You're obviously a high achiever and have done very well at both school and university, but except for a week at your local council, you don't have any administrative experience. Why, if politics is your ambition, have you not gained more practical experience in your free time?"

The young woman flushed. "My parents felt that study should be my main priority." Wanting more, the interviewer leaned forward. Glowing scarlet, the girl continued, "And then in the holidays I'd have to help in the shop and at home with my younger brothers and sisters." She forced a laugh. "Everyone has a job to do in our family. It only works if we all do our bit." The thin woman leaned back, picked up her pen and made some notes.

"We tend to have a lot of tight deadlines." The man was speaking again. "If you knew you couldn't make a deadline, what would you do?"

"I would meet the deadline, if I had to. I would definitely meet the deadline." Grinning, she relaxed.

"But if you couldn't, what steps would you take?"

She frowned, looked at his face and pursed her lips together in thought. He made little nods of his head. "I just would. I've never missed a deadline, no matter what I had to do. I once stayed up for forty-eight hours to meet my end-of-term deadlines."

There was silence, then the man said, "You're not alone here, there is quite a lot of support. So what other resources do you think you could use to manage your workload, if you weren't going to meet a deadline?"

She shook her head. "I'd make the deadline, I really would." He kept nodding. The other silent man wrote on his pad.

They shook her hand, one after the other, and thanked her for coming. "We'll make our decision by the twenty-third and notify you by letter."

The three interviewers sat at the table looking over their notes. They glanced at one another and the middle-aged man spoke first.

"She was by far the best candidate. The way she talked about working together with communities would make her a great asset."

Nodding in agreement, the woman replied, "I feel the same, but she didn't answer the questions in the way required by the regulations. And this hiring will be scrutinised so there's no wiggle room." She looked at the quiet director, faintly quizzical; he gazed back impassively.

The director then stood up. "I'll leave you both to it."

The thin woman waited for the door to close behind him and continued, "It's a shame. The young man knew how to respond—he was quite slick—but I suspect communities isn't his priority."

"It's not orthodox, but I'll invite the young woman to apply for an internship. I don't want to see potential go to waste. She needs to get her foot in the door. Once she's in, I think she's got what it takes to make a real difference."

"Good idea."

"Just doing what I can."

They smiled at each other as he stacked his files together.

"Although it doesn't change the fact that our chosen

candidate will be on your team, so you'll bear the brunt," she added.

"Don't I know it." As he marched from the room, his smile disappeared.

"I want to deal with this now," he growled, standing next to his supervisor's desk, vibrating with rage. "Grace made her complaint the moment I'd stepped away from my desk for the interviews."

The supervisor finished typing her sentence. "Give me an hour. I need to finish this report." She didn't look at him.

"Now. I've been accused of bullying. I won't wait."

In silence, she pushed back from her desk and, with the eyes of the entire workforce upon them, they crossed the open plan office to a meeting room. He closed the door behind them.

"Grace feels that you're often abrupt and that you overload her with unrealistic deadlines."

"Are you kidding me? That woman does nothing all day—when I ask her to do something she always makes an excuse or ignores me."

"I realise there are problems with Grace's productivity, but what you have to do is let me deal with it through the correct procedures."

"I'm not the only one who's complained about her. So all these correct procedures aren't making a damn bit of difference. I've three or four deadlines every day and I can't ask the admin assistant for support?!"

"Which is why you need to let me deal with it. Grace wants you to write an apology to show that you recognise her feelings."

"An apology! That woman gets paid to sit around all day and I have to apologise to her. In writing."

"We need to work together on this and smooth ruffled feathers. It's in all our best interests to deal with it and move on. I'll write the apology for you and then all you have to do is agree to the content—"

He interrupted her. "No way. I'm not apologising for bullying. I don't bully her. I just ask her to do her job." He had raised his voice to a shout. "And I'm not having the word 'bullying' on my record. Fuck that." He stomped back to his desk, with his supervisor following with a measured step. Eyes were still on them.

He looked at his watch: 3:40. Picking up his bag and without turning off his computer, he walked away from his desk. Ignoring him, his supervisor continued to stare at her screen. A few people muttered goodbyes from behind their desks.

"Off early?" the director laughed, as they passed one another in the corridor. He stopped laughing and added, "You okay?"

"A migraine," he responded.

"Feel better. I'll see you at the departmental meeting on Friday morning. Oh, I realise it's short notice, but can you get me the report on the south-east green spaces by midday Thursday?

"Thursday! Okay, okay, of course." He rubbed his head as the director continued.

"And sorry again about how the interviews went: the arrogance of youth will soon be knocked out of him when reality kicks in. I'm sure you'll whip him into shape in no time—if anyone can, you can. Also, about Grace: I want to reassure you we are working to resolve the situation."

"I'm so sorry, I'm all over the place." The woman had freckles dotted across her nose. They both bent down to pick up their broken glasses.

"Don't worry about that, mate. I'll clear it up." Emerging from behind the bar, the attendant began loading the broken glass into a bucket.

"Can I get you another drink?" offered the middle-aged man, politely.

"Thank you," she accepted.

"The usual and a glass of red, please." The landlord poured the wine and the woman withdrew, thanking them both, and returned to her table where her friend sat looking concerned.

"You're early today." The landlord pulled down on the pump.

"I'm sick of it. The civil service is full of fucking free-loaders. It makes me apoplectic with rage, and it's the taxpayer who suffers." He was shouting. "And you can't get rid of these fuckers because of the procedures. It's fucking outrageous. And I'm the one accused of bullying. The director had better be true to his word. If not, I'll take it into my own hands." The landlord placed the pint in front of the man.

"There you go mate, that'll sort you out."

"There are five triggers, that's what the leaflet says. Here, I'll show you." Her eyes filled with tears as she searched in her bag and pulled out a handful of papers. A letter sat on top:

Hospital admission: 9:00 a.m., 23rd May, Addington Ward

Tears dripped onto the papers as she fumbled through them. Holding her gently by the wrists, her friend stopped her fevered motions. "It's okay." Removing the papers from her grasp, she returned them to her friend's bag. "We're supposed to be drinking to forget. Remember?" Holding up her glass she said, "To friendship!" and took a swig.

The freckle-faced woman lifted her glass but was unable to drink. Her face crumpled and again she started to cry. "You'll come to the hospital for the operation, won't you? Please."

"I'm insulted you have to ask. Of course I'll be there," the friend replied, and reached across the table to stroke her hand. "I'd take this away for you if I could, but I can't. I can make sure you're not alone, though."

"Thank you." The freckle-faced woman gripped her friend's hand and for a moment the tension eased.

"Now drink." Following her friend's instruction the freckle-faced woman forced herself to drink and gulped at her wine. The music changed. "I love this song, it's a tune!" She shouted the word 'tune'. Pushing tables aside and jumping in the air, she held her arms up, punching her fists towards the ceiling. She leaped to the beat of the music. Joining her on the makeshift dance floor, her friend shook her long hair and repeatedly jolted her head forward, headbanging. Together they played air guitar and air drums. Men watched. The man whose beer she'd knocked over joined them, headbanging and playing imaginary guitar. They laughed together. Separating the friends, he moved towards the freckle-faced woman and slipped his hands on her hips. Over his shoulder, she opened her eyes in accentuated surprise. Her friend put both of her thumbs up and mouthed the words, "Go for it!"

Forcing her mouth on his, the freckle-faced woman gave the man a frantic kiss. He withdrew and wiped his mouth. She laughed too hard. "Do you want to feel my cancer tits?" she offered and placed his hands on her breasts. Sliding his hands away from her chest and down her arms, he squeezed her hands tightly.

He said, "My sister had breast cancer and it was tough, but now she's okay. You can get through this."

Half laughing through her tears, she clung onto him and he let her. They swayed gently together for a few moments. When they finally disengaged, she looked up at his face. "Thank you, I mean, sorry about that, but thank you." He kissed her on the cheek.

"Make sure you don't leave her," he said to her friend and walked away.

"This train is ready to depart. Please mind the doors." Beeping sounded a warning, and a moment before the doors closed, two women ran onto the carriage, one slightly ahead of the other. Sitting down on the seats diagonally opposite him, a freckle-faced woman beckoned for her friend to join her.

The young man examined his phone.

How did the interview go, old chap?

He tapped out a reply:

Exceptionally well. Thanks for the insider tips. I knew the answer to every question before they'd even finished asking it! I may be a council-estate prole but I've put the work in, and I'll make it all the way to the foreign office, and who knows from there.

He pressed send. A low buzz of voices reverberated around the carriage. Frequently he heard an outburst of laughter or one side of a conversation. Next to him a man took a large bite from a burger and chewed it with a noisy smacking of lips. The station sign began to gently slip past him and soon the Houses of Parliament emerged. Hundreds of lights were reflected off the river.

Scrolling down the screen of his phone, he passed over pictures of pets and memes advocating that a little kindness goes a long way. He read the headlines of articles and videos people had posted. Ignoring 'List of Arrested Journalists in Turkey' and 'Chechnya Planning to Eliminate Gay People from Region', he stopped and read the post of a distant friend under the headline 'How the Election Split France. No surprises: the rural poor voted for the Nazi-wannabe. The urban educated did not.' He pressed 'comment' and typed:

Being part of the Front National doesn't mean being a Nazi. It's a different political group. Do you think the rural poor are unable to make reasonable judgments just because they're poor? I think you underestimate us financially challenged individuals.

He pressed send and continued reading. He stopped at a black-and-white photo of two men standing in a ditch. They were in the desert and both leaned on shovels, sporting pith helmets and moustaches. Under 'Exploring the Depths and Heights of Ancient Egypt', he typed:

There's nothing exciting left to discover now: it's all been done. Born in the wrong era and wrong class, my dear chap. It's a shame—we would have made excellent wealthy Victorians and explored the far reaches of the globe.

Sitting bolt upright, the freckle-faced woman clamped her hand over her mouth. "I'm going to be sick," she warned her friend through closed fingers. Before her friend had a chance to respond, the woman vomited between her legs and onto the floor. He watched them. The train was nearly empty and there were rumpled fast-food wrappings and newspapers strewn across the floors and over the seats. With one hand he held a handkerchief over his mouth, gagging, and with his other hand offered the friend his spare handkerchief from the top pocket of his jacket, and then his bottle of water.

"Thank you, you're a lifesaver," she said, as the freckle-faced woman vomited again. He turned away and walked down the carriage. Huddling around a phone, three teenage boys watched a music video. The train slowed as it approached his station. He stared at his reflection in the window of the train doors.

"I'm gonna blow your brains out." The young man turned to see the tallest boy pointing a handgun directly at his head. Behind him, the other two jeered.

"Not with that fake gun you're not." Turning away from them, he saw three figures crowd his reflection and witnessed himself kicked to the ground. Faces stared down at him, contorted by physical effort. One foot after another slammed into his body. A heavy boot stamped down on his shoulder, stomach and hips in turn. Holding his umbrella in his left hand, he rolled onto his right side. The blows continuing, he placed his right hand on the floor; the boot crushed his fingers but he pushed against it and, with his other hand, he used the umbrella as a lever and began to raise himself up from the floor. He jabbed an elbow out and the foot on his hand lifted. Punches pounded his ear and his back. He managed to get up. Hitting out with the umbrella, he attacked in any way possible, with all the power he had. He slugged with his right and stabbed with his left, and kicked out, hard. Forced against the train doors, he fell onto the platform as they opened. He rolled to his feet and ran. Blood flowed from his nose. His umbrella was destroyed; metal spikes jutted at sharp angles and the fabric was shredded.

Once safe, he stopped and leaned over, hands on his knees, to recover his breath. As he slowly stood up, he felt the pain of his injuries throughout his body and wiped the blood off with his sleeve. He put the umbrella into a bin, rolled his shoulders back and dusted off his suit. He grinned.

"Excuse me, is this yours?" When he turned around, the woman he had given the water to was holding out a wallet. He patted his pockets.

"Yes, I didn't realise it had fallen out. Thank you—now you're the lifesaver." They exchanged smiles.

"I hate to ask, but could you help me get my friend through the barrier? She's out of her noggin."

She indicated to the freckle-faced woman, who was crawling up the platform and shouting, "Mum! I want my mum!"

Together they lifted the sagging woman, one on each arm, and half marched, half dragged her to the barrier. The sober woman went through first and waited on the other side of the gate. He held up the protesting woman from behind and, as the gate opened, pushed her past the barrier into the arms of her friend. When all three were beyond the platform, they linked arms and struggled to a nearby bench.

"Can I help with anything else?" he asked.

"I wanna give you a kiss." The freckle-faced woman lunged forward, her lips puckered up ready for kissing. Her friend held her back on the bench.

"No, thank you, we've got a cab coming. But thanks a million. I'd never have managed on my own." She wrestled to keep her friend upright.

"It is a privilege; I couldn't leave two damsels in distress." He made a small bow. "If that's all, I'll be on my merry way."

As he strolled, the shouts of the drunken woman still audible, he quietly sang a Beatles favourite to himself.

... *five six seven eight nine ten, I love you. All together now, all together now ...*

Half Life

From the day Adelaide Anderson was diagnosed, it took three years, two months, one week and four days for her to die. She was thirty-six.

—◦◦◦—

Adelaide had told her husband and sister she would haunt them if she had the chance. She had said this sitting in the overcrowded phlebotomy waiting room, immediately after the news that her condition was possibly terminal. The consultant, Dr. Wells, had said it would be difficult for Adelaide to think of anything but the worst-case scenario, but she should nonetheless focus on the fact that the outcome wasn't certain. After her declaration to become a ghost, her sister had given a nervous half-laugh and said that she didn't want Adelaide to do anything to scare her. Adelaide had agreed, but said she'd move things around her home just to confuse her. And laughed too. Her husband, Simon, had told her not to be morbid and reminded her that the consultant wasn't sure. It was possible she might live.

Everything in the house was a perfect reproduction of her family home, alike enough to have been the actual house. As she walked from room to room, alternately calling for her sister, brother and parents, Hector, her pet cat, began following her. Relieved at his company, she knelt down and stroked his head. He purred under her touch. It seemed so natural to bend down, but it had been a long time since she'd been able to move. Luxuriating in her actions, she ran her hand over his body. Hector had been dead for at least ten years. She'd been devastated at the time. Nothing was clear to her about how she came to be in the house or why. She had no memory of entering. Calling for her family was a vain hope; she knew she was alone. They were not dead.

Adelaide had spent the week following her consultant's appointment panicking—crying and screaming as if the pain were physical. Unable to calm herself, she'd stand in the kitchen attempting to draw breath and clasping onto her sister's arms to steady herself. She couldn't be alone. Alarmed at her behaviour, Imogen tried to soothe her.

"They have to tell you the worst-case scenario, Ade, to be sure, to cover themselves." Adelaide shook her head with frantic movements, denying that was the case.

"You were there, you saw how serious she was." And

the panic would start again, with Adelaide repeating, "I can't believe it, I can't believe it, I can't believe it."

She couldn't eat for fear that being unable to swallow would confirm the diagnosis. At night she clung onto Simon, crying as he reassured her.

"Let's just take one day at a time."

He'd lure her to sleep only for her to jolt awake at the remembrance of her situation, and she would cry again. This process continued for weeks, until the idea of dying settled on her like a toxic dust. Death became part of her normal, everyday thoughts and panic was reduced to regular intervals.

Although the house was her family home, it contained none of the paraphernalia of human life. It was unnaturally clean. Every surface was clear, the usual piles of paperwork were absent and the jumbled drawers of junk collected as "things we might need in the future" were tidy. No shoes loitered at the bottom of the stairs. It was like a show home. Her bedroom still had the bunk beds she had shared with Imogen, but the top bed was made with such precision not a crease was visible on the duvet. Her cosmetics and toiletries were laid out in rows on her dressing table and her wardrobe was full of clothes that hung one item to a hanger. She sat on her bed and beckoned Hector to come and sit with her. When she'd shared a room with her sister she'd tried any amount of nagging, violence or bribery to get Imogen to leave her things as she'd wanted them, but now the neatness felt cold. Her sister should bounce through the door, climb onto her bed and demand to wear Adelaide's new top just because she felt entitled to it.

At work her boss hadn't been especially sympathetic, at least not in the beginning. If she needed time off for appointments she was expected to work extra hours and make up the time. But then she hadn't actually told her boss how serious things were. Adelaide had worked in her local library for eight years. As a sixth former she'd completed her two weeks' work experience at the British Library, and decided that's what she wanted to do. Following an obvious path as an undergraduate, she studied English literature and history, and then went on to complete a master's degree in library studies. At some point her plan to work at the British Library, or in a specialist collection, subsided and she accepted that one's desires didn't always come to fruition. After her initial ambition faded, working in the local library satisfied her. It wasn't exactly exciting but she believed that she had a moderate amount of talent and intelligence and that was reflected in her situation. She was content to organise local book groups and help individuals with their information needs. Until now. Looking to her past gave her a feeling of vertigo: she'd wasted so much time. Questioning every choice she'd made throughout her life, she regretted settling for what had come easily. She'd failed to seize opportunities for excitement, pleasure and advancement.

Her decision not to share her health issues at this stage

was a practical one. There was little point in discussing it and making false claims before she was fully diagnosed.

Adelaide made one exception. She'd been friends with Bret for five years, ever since he'd come to work at the library. Mostly they laughed together, sharing an almost puerile sense of humour, and she'd told him without reserve details about her life. They had a casual intimacy. He sometimes had strange beliefs, and Adelaide suspected he had a secret sadness he couldn't confess. To counter this, he'd follow whatever self-help or spiritual trend was in fashion. His current fad was Kabbalah.

"Honestly, Ade, I've met people whose lives have been totally transformed after they start going to the meetings. It's a great focus." His enthusiasm never failed, no matter how many times he started over with a new belief. This one even had an answer to her problem. "There was a man who had stomach cancer; he joined Kabbalah and stayed up all night meditating with his group. By the morning he was cured." This was incredible, even by Bret's standards.

"So you're suggesting if I meditate all night I'll cure my nerve damage?"

"It's worth a go." He shrugged.

"You do realise how serious nerve damage is?"

"So is cancer. Can't make it any worse. Come along to a meeting." Adelaide couldn't handle Bret's illogical, blind belief, and that desperate people were taken in by such ideas made her furious. Her initial instinct to keep her condition to herself had been right.

the word her mind picked out as the sound of the machine started up. Together the radio and machine created a discordant cacophony. *Pissh, comm, pissh, comm, pissh, comm.* The machine sounded like an electronic imitation of a steam engine. It was overwhelming. Being physically constrained and trapped, coupled with the intense noise, frightened her. Her head was held in place by a brace. Banging surrounded her. It continued in a regular rhythm as if someone with a hammer was desperate to break in. Without notice, the banging changed to a screech. The mechanical beast was in pain. On occasion the bed would jolt forward and readjust for the next round of images. The interior entombed her, the top lingering only a few inches away from her face. Adelaide closed her eyes and recited the C scale. And then recited it again. Repeating it kept the panic at bay. She'd been learning the piano for just over a year and had recently taken her Grade 1 exam. Being able to play an instrument had been one of her ambitions since childhood. Although she'd tried a few times it had never stuck. At last she was making progress and could see a time when she'd be able to play well. She loved it; proud of what she'd achieved. But it had been her music teacher who had pointed out her fingers hadn't strengthened; in fact, her thumbs were getting weaker. Unable to face giving up, she'd kept going as long as her fingers had allowed. She was to have three scans, each taking twenty minutes. Keeping her eyes tight shut she continued reciting her scales and blocking out the cycle of changing sounds, each more alarming than the last.

"It's perfect, Adelaide." Imogen was staring at the screen.

Adelaide was surprised at how well formed the baby was. Each part of it was clearly definable. She'd had no idea that babies were so well developed at twenty weeks of growth. The black-and-white screen illuminated Imogen and Jack's beaming faces.

"Would you like to know the sex?" the sonographer asked. Imogen laughed.

"You have to keep it secret, Ade."

"Of course, what do you take me for?" Adelaide pretended to be offended. The sonographer pushed the probe over her sister's protruding belly. They all stared at the screen.

"The baby's got its leg in the way. Sorry, I can't see." Imogen lightly tapped her stomach and the baby shifted its position. "You've got it trained already." The sonographer laughed as she repositioned the probe. After a pause she announced, "It's a girl. There" She pointed to the screen. "You can you see the vagina." Imogen was grinning.

"Wonderful." She kissed Jack. "I've always wanted a girl."

Adelaide hadn't even thought about wanting a baby. She was thirty-three and had imagined there'd be plenty of time to consider having a family. Her sister was creating life and hers might be coming to an end. For the first time, she felt dislocated from Imogen.

Trapped in the house but no longer trapped in her body, Adelaide ran around, relishing every step. Forgetting things on purpose gave her an excuse to run upstairs and fetch them. And bathing everyday meant she could enjoy climbing in and out of the bath. Initially, she was unsure of how her body would function, but during the first few days it became obvious she still became hungry and tired in the same way. When she was alive and in full health she'd cycled everywhere. Sometimes she felt like the perfect stereotype of a librarian, slowly cycling to and from work, taking things at her own pace. Her bicycle had a traditional frame in a beautiful deep green. It was the freedom and independence that cycling gave her that she most enjoyed. By the power of her own body, she could get to where she needed to go, never having to wait for public transport. She'd only given up when she could no longer lift her leg high enough to step over the frame.

Unable to leave the house, she obviously couldn't cycle, but she could roller-skate. The Christmas before Adelaide left home, Imogen had bought her a pair of rainbow-coloured roller boots. They had bright red wheels and she'd chosen them because they resembled a pair she'd owned as a child. It was their joint plan to resurrect a much-loved hobby. However, on their first outing Adelaide, attempting to show off, had skated backwards around a bend at high speed, lost her footing and crashed into a stationary car, knocking herself out. After that the skates had been dumped in the cupboard under the stairs and left for dead.

The skates were still there. Adelaide took a risk that the neighbours couldn't leave their houses either and turned up the stereo as loud as it would go. The laminate flooring was the ideal surface for a roller disco. At first she wobbled and held onto the dining chairs, but soon she was able to cross the room, and by the end of the third song she considered herself a resurrected dancing queen. She laughed aloud, dancing and spinning.

"The skates aren't wasted now, Imogen." She stopped and looked around the room at the door, half hoping Imogen would walk through it. She turned off the music. The house was silent.

The refuge of expecting the worst wasn't enough to keep her safe. Hope, fragmented and transitory, kept breaking into her thoughts. Hundreds of times she entered her symptoms into the search engine and trawled the results for any condition that contradicted the current theory. She searched until she found a benign explanation. This gave her a respite. Once again she had a future, again the luxury of wasting time and basking in the feeling that life could be taken for granted. In these periods, the thought that she was having tests was a comfort. At the least, it meant that there was reasonable doubt she wasn't dying. One evening, after her regular choir practice, her toes clipped the edge of a raised cobblestone and she fell in the middle of the road in front of a busy theatre. The crowd queuing up for the performance stared at her. People were confused when she called for help. Adelaide was scared the lights would change and the traffic begin to flow. A couple in smart business clothes stepped forward.

"Are you hurt?" the woman asked. They both looked worried for her.

"I can't get up. I can't get up. I don't have the strength." Increasing panic intensified her voice. As the man attempted to pull her from the ground, he was surprised at encountering her dead weight. Adelaide clung to him as he lifted her, her face pushing against his chest and her legs limp. She smelled his mix of sweat and cologne. The woman stared at them, frowning as she watched their awkward wrestling. She clutched at Adelaide's bag. When Adelaide was on her feet, she was embarrassed. "So sorry. Sorry, thank you, thank you." Retrieving her bag from the woman, she continued to apologise and limped to the side of the road. The couple stared after her.

"Are you sure you're okay? Is there anything we can do?" Adelaide didn't want to cry in front of them.

"No, thank you, I'm fine, honestly. Thank you." She walked with slow deliberate steps and, as she turned the corner, allowed herself to cry. Shocked and hurt, she limped towards the bus stop. Her knee had been twisted and the skin on her hand was broken and bloody. But it was the realisation of how vulnerable she had become that terrified her.

Once again, the skates were enshrined under the stairs. The novelty of being able to move again had begun to wane; not that she wasn't pleased, but it was becoming normal. Distraction techniques were something she'd have to develop but at least she had plenty to do. The TV worked, there was a vast DVD collection and loads of books. Books had been a central part of her life and her parents had allowed her to create a library in the living room. She suspected her dad secretly passed the books off as his own to make himself look educated. Both of her parents worked in office jobs, her father for an insurance firm and her mother at the local council. Neither of them had been to university and as far back as she could remember her father's advice had been to stay at school or college as long as possible. It had less to do with getting an education than work being a lifelong burden.

Photographs of Thomas, Imogen and Adelaide in their graduation gowns all glared down from the shelf. Thomas was four years older than her and had gone off to university when she was in Year 10. Since that time he had hardly spent any time at home. He was either on a work placement abroad or away with friends, and then in his first job he met his girlfriend. During Adelaide's illness he had sent her flowers and the odd text, but she'd only seen him a few times. He was ambitious and self-contained. Once he'd decided on the life he wanted, he fully committed to it with an intensity that Adelaide admired. He'd had his own company by the time he was twenty-six and travelled all over the world. The rest of the family, no longer a crucial part of his existence, joked he must have been switched at birth. She envied his direction and drive, wishing she had been equally ambitious.

Scanning the shelves, she looked for books she hadn't read. They were usually the long, challenging classics, which would take time and fortitude to finish: *Don Quixote*, *David Copperfield* and *War and Peace*. She now had plenty of time. Pulling *War and Peace* from the shelf, she flicked through it. The pages were bare. She checked *Don Quixote*; again, the pages were empty. Frantic, Adelaide fumbled through the pages of *Vanity Fair*. This was one of her favourite novels; the pages were intact. Working along the shelves, Adelaide looked through the pages of every book. All of the books she hadn't read had blank pages.

Slumped on the sofa, Adelaide turned on the television. She pressed play on the remote and waited for the DVD to work. Again, any film she hadn't seen produced a fuzzy black-and-white screen. Flicking through the channels was a futile act; she knew that anything she could watch she would already have seen. Adelaide was stuck in a world of repeats and rereads. Hector jumped up and snuggled next to her, watching as she ate her ever-replenishing supply of hot dogs. She offered him a piece, but he sniffed it and left it uneaten on the cushion. There was some consolation in her comfort food and Hector's adoration. But this odd half life had no explanation or logic.

When she woke up a youth panel show was blaring out from the television; young, attractive people mocked each other about their choice of funny videos picked from YouTube. She remembered having seen this when she'd been staying in a hotel alone. Nervous at sleeping away from home, she'd kept the TV on all night. Blue light from the screen flickered and it was cold. Hector had moved onto her lap to keep warm. Her feet were freezing and she noticed a strong breeze coming from the hallway. Removing Hector, she leaned forward to see where the draft could be coming from. The front door was wide open.

Adelaide was intrigued at the variety of tests she had to go through. After the claustrophobia of the MRI scan came a lumber puncture. The information leaflet made it sound gruesome. A local anaesthetic would be administered to the lower back and then a needle inserted into the spine and fluid extracted. Adelaide wasn't afraid of needles in particular, but the idea of having her spine tampered with made her uncomfortable. In the waiting room she looked at the other people there and wondered what might be wrong with them. There was an elderly couple and the woman looked frail, with her bony fingers and ghoulishly translucent skin. An engagement ring, heavy with a large diamond, hung limp and loose on her left hand. She clung onto a folder that was full of what looked to Adelaide like appointment letters. A middle-aged man, plump in the face and round-bellied, flicked through a lifestyle magazine. On the television a quizmaster asked quick-fire questions. Adelaide tried to answer and the plump-faced man joined in, and they laughed when they answered a question wrong. After the quiz show, a couple were shown around country homes to see if any met their ideal of rural living. Everything appeared to be so normal. She must appear normal to those she shared the waiting room with. After forty minutes, Adelaide was invited into a treatment room. The doctor carried her bag as he apologised for the late running of the clinic.

"It's been mad here this morning," he told them. Adelaide was convinced he'd carried the bag because he knew how bad things were for her.

"Just take your shoes off, loosen your clothes so I can get access to your lower back, and pop yourself up here on the bed." He had dark curls and spoke in a gentle voice. The light was too bright, making everything look harsh and stark.

"The procedure sounds worse than it is. The anaesthetic is the most painful part." It stung, but that only lasted a few moments. "It won't take long to feel the effect. Lie still, I'll be back in a minute." She was lying on her side in a foetal position. Simon sat in front of her, holding her hand.

"Don't worry, it will be over soon." He kissed her cheek. The rest of the procedure was easy. She couldn't see what the doctor was doing and couldn't feel it.

"Over. I told you it sounds worse than it is. I just need to get the nurse to do some special bloods that Dr. Wells has requested. You need to rest for half an hour anyway; it takes a little while for the spinal fluid to get back to normal." He disappeared through the curtain, taking the sample with him.

"Special bloods. Jesus. What do you think that means?" Adelaide was actually pleased. It might mean that the consultant had thought of some lesser disease, one which might not mean death.

The flat was in a state of disarray and there were half-packed boxes in all of the rooms, except for the kitchen, which had been packed up entirely. Simon and Adelaide had lived in this flat for seven years. She'd loved it, and although it was small, she'd enjoyed making the most of all the space. Wherever a shelf could be built, she'd put one in, and had even designed a perfectly snug work unit and library in the spare room.

In their bedroom, the duvet was crumpled into a ball and sat in the centre of the mattress. The clock showed her the time and date. It had been nearly three months since her death. Time no longer made sense; she'd only been in the house for a week. Simon would be at work now and she longed to see him. Their half-empty home reminded her of when they'd moved in and had expected to spend a lifetime together.

A grey dim light made the living room seem cold. She walked to the window. Rain fell and a large puddle had collected in the gutter directly in front of the building. Standing in the tiny garden there was a "For Sale" sign, but "Sold" blocked out the words. He obviously didn't feel the need to stay in their home to remind him of her and relive memories of their life together. That's what she'd have done. Or maybe he was moving because it was too sad for him to remain. This explanation appeased her, making her still feel loved. But after another moment, anger overwhelmed her. It was so hurtful. He hadn't cared at all. If he had, then he couldn't even think about moving. Moving on.

Adelaide wanted to find him, go to his office and see him, try to ask him if he'd really loved her. But she was in another life where she didn't know the rules. She didn't know if she could see other people, or them her, or if she could travel as normal. There was only one way to find out.

Opening the flat door she walked through the frame.

Once again she stood in the hallway of her childhood home. Hector trotted up and sat at her feet.

"Come in, don't be shy. I'm Dr. Pym." The consultant neurophysiologist thrust out a rough hand. Adelaide offered hers in return and it was engulfed by a double-handed grasp.

"Ms. Anderson, sit on the bed. There are some chairs over there." He indicated to a blue adjustable bed and some plastic chairs. Simon lifted a chair from the pile and placed it next to the bed. On the other side of the room sat a serious-looking young woman. "This is Dr. Khan; she's training. You don't mind her sitting in, do you?"

"Of course not, everyone needs to learn." Adelaide smiled at the straight-faced trainee doctor. She nodded back in acknowledgment.

"Okay, so what have we got here today?" Dr. Pym was pawing through her medical notes. Adelaide was aghast that he didn't already know. But then decided that it was a good sign; she was low priority, of lesser importance, not needing the attention of a busy consultant. It was all good. He spent a few moments turning pages back and forth and making the occasional grunt. He addressed Dr. Khan. "Seems distal at the moment." Again Dr. Khan nodded and then got up and stood in front of Adelaide.

"Do you mind?" She asked Dr. Pym, not Adelaide.

"Not at all. Go ahead."

"Lift up your arm." Dr. Khan began to perform the standard neurological tests. By this time Adelaide knew the tests well, but she would have preferred it if Dr. Khan had asked her. She felt like public property. Being ill seemed to mean anyone could invade your personal space. The intrusion of the trainee had been too spontaneously assertive and it unbalanced Adelaide's notion of how an appointment should proceed.

"It's not the tests I'm afraid of, it's the results." Adelaide forced a laugh.

Dr. Khan pushed down flat on Adelaide's elevated elbow; it gave way and settled about halfway between her shoulder and side.

"Three." Moving to her hands, she interlocked their fingers. "Grip as hard as you can." Adelaide complied.

"Four. Now pull up as hard as you can." Dr. Khan had her wrist against Adelaide's. She pulled. "Three."

"Okay. Thank you, good work." Dr. Pym flipped through the file one more time. Looking at the file pages, he commented to no one in particular, "Looks like Dr. Wells has some ideas about your diagnosis. Not very optimistic, but then anyone who ends up at her clinic knows the outlook's bad."

Stunned by the truth presented with such casual brutality, Adelaide sat there, silent.

Imogen and Elinor sat at the dining room table having lunch. Elinor had two bear-shaped snacks and they were chatting, giving Imogen a performance. Adelaide stood watching them, transfixed. A relief that she had never felt before lightened her body, as if she were in love. She laughed as Elinor bit the head off one of the bears. They all laughed and for a moment Adelaide felt they were all sharing the joke together. Normality had been restored. The dining room was as she remembered it. The shelf full of miniature flamingoes was a shock of pink. Imogen had a lifelong fondness for flamingoes. The doorbell rang.

"Come in. It's just through the living room." Imogen followed the collection driver and his assistant. Adelaide was sitting in Imogen's chair next to Elinor. They watched as Imogen led the men, or rather the man and his teen-age companion, who looked as if he wouldn't be able to lift a dustpan and brush, through to the extension. The extension had been built to accommodate Adelaide when she'd been too weak to manage. Simon had agreed that she should move out of their flat and into Imogen's house. He had kind of moved in, living out of his suitcase, his clean laundry dumped in one corner of the room, his dirty laundry in the other.

She wasn't sure how she'd feel at seeing the room again and followed Imogen with caution. Her first impression was how light it was. The far wall, which led out onto the garden, was entirely glass. She remembered how she'd loved watching the birds come and go. It had kept her amused for hours. At dusk, she'd been lulled to sleep by the rhythmic cooing of the wood pigeons. The men worked with speed, disassembling her bed.

Simon had hardly shown his emotions throughout her illness, but one evening he'd sat on the edge of her bed, feeding her dinner, and she'd commented that it wasn't the worst thing, being looked after.

"No, being without you is the worst thing. A hundred years with you wouldn't be enough." Then he'd cried and hugged her tight. But within two minutes he'd dried his eyes and continued feeding her.

There was already a piano in the room. It had been the plan to make it into a music room. There was a picture of her and Imogen on the top of it. They were wearing their glad rags and most glamorous makeup. It had been taken at their cousin's wedding and they were hugging, their cheeks pushed together. They looked happy. Adelaide couldn't believe this had been taken only a year before she'd become ill. She laid her fingers on the keys; she longed to play. She'd thought she'd be a role model to Elinor, encouraging her in her musical endeavours, and had imagined playing duets together. She'd also thought they'd have sleepovers and go to the seaside. At least she could spend time with her now, even if Elinor wasn't aware of it.

Adelaide followed the teenager as he clung onto the back end of the mattress and edged it through into the living room. Elinor had finished her lunch and was forcing her feet into a pair of wellies. Imogen returned from showing the removers out. She wiped tears from her eyes and blew her nose.

"Now that's all over we can get on with things again. Do you want to help Mummy with some gardening?" Elinor nodded her head up and down. Imogen pulled back the patio door and Elinor ran out into the garden. It was a joy to see her. Adelaide followed Imogen through the garden door and was again back in the hallway of her old home.

Now that the diagnosis was official it was as if she was being initiated into a secret club. In one morning she saw a physiotherapist, a wheelchair occupational therapist, met the clinic secretary and had a consultation with a specialist nurse.

"Most people are just relieved to know what's wrong with them," one of them said in a professionally caring tone. If she'd just been told she had an overactive thyroid or a broken leg she would be inclined to agree. But to be told at thirty-three that she had a massively reduced life span didn't coincide with what she considered a relief.

It was also hard to remember she wouldn't die as she was. Although weak, she could still walk, stand up with a struggle and climb stairs, albeit slowly. If she could halt the disease at this point she'd cope. Disability was preferable to death. Adelaide was pacified by the idea that at the time of her death, she'd be so fed up with being ill, she'd be happy to die. However, it abhorred her to imagine that anyone would say, "It's better she's gone and out of her misery." It would be better not to have been ill at all. Obviously.

Everything about life had changed. Her assumptions about her future had been destroyed. Gone was the "positive illusion" of a predictable and controllable world. She'd never get old and her parents would outlive her. Nothing made sense. People around her looked alien, were alien. Their experience no longer coincided with hers and she felt outside of everyday pleasures, ordinary worries and trivial concerns.

Adelaide was frightened to be alone but alienated from people who didn't know what was happening to her. It was difficult to chat about holidays and future plans, while keeping the abyss that faced her a secret. When she did confide in others she found she continued to be lonely. People didn't find it easy to hang out with someone who had just told them they were going to die. Plus, it was difficult to cope with their reactions. Some people became upset, and some who wouldn't cry if she'd died, cried to hear she was going to die. Of course, Adelaide was aware they were crying partly for the shadow cast over their own mortality, but she kept quiet, watching the security of their lives crumble.

More people than Adelaide would have guessed reacted by underplaying her illness. Some said, "Well, we've all got to die sometime"; others, "None of us know how long we have"; and the most clichéd, "I could get run over by a bus tomorrow." Confused and angered, she'd often reply that she could see her bus coming up the road and couldn't get out of the way, while theirs was still parked at the depot. She never felt guilty about frightening them. It was exactly because their own deaths were abstract that they could say such things.

Adelaide felt that no one should know when they were going to die. Often she'd watch people cross the road, weaving between the cars without concern for their lives. If they were given a terminal diagnosis, they'd be devastated, but without it thought nothing of risking their lives on a daily basis.

Although she didn't want to, Adelaide realised that

191

she would have to take responsibility for how people treated her. If she was upset, she'd explain she didn't need solutions or cheering up, but just wanted some sympathy. If she wanted to express how unfair it was or how grief-stricken she was, she didn't need unrealistic optimism, only an acknowledgment of how sad she was. Eventually, she wanted to scream at people not to waste their time and to embrace existence with all their energy. Waiting for the conditions of life to be perfect was pointless; if you couldn't afford ten days in the Bahamas, then a weekend at Camber Sands would be enough.

At work she'd decided to tell her boss the whole story. Her symptoms still weren't obvious and she'd managed to avoid lifting piles of books and using the ladders. She often volunteered to help library users with difficult enquiries so her absences from the physical work weren't too obvious. But she kept crying, unable to contain her grief. At these moments she'd repeat to herself, "I'm going to die." Her colleagues were sure to notice something was wrong.

Donna was sympathetic when she heard the diagnosis. She listened when Adelaide shared her fears and allowed her to talk about her situation over and over, as if talking could make it right again. Adelaide would cry and wasn't ashamed, feeling that Donna had invited her to confide. Donna's own sister had died the previous year. They'd been close and it had taken her three months to get back to work full-time. As assistant manager, it had been Adelaide's job to take responsibility and make sure everything was running smoothly. She'd been happy to do it. To Adelaide, losing her sister was one of the worst things she could imagine. Supporting Donna through her loss was the least she could do. And now Donna was supporting her.

"I'll put you on light duties, but the one thing I ask of you is don't cry in front of the library users. If you're feeling overwhelmed just let me know and we can pull you off the front desk."

Adelaide was grateful. She wanted to stay at work as long as possible. Being home alone would be unbearable, giving her too much time to think about her situation.

Bret's unsympathetic reaction to her potential diagnosis had meant she'd avoided him as much as possible but now she missed him and felt sure that her certain death would have some impact.

"Healing works on an emotional and spiritual level, Ade. I know it's not popular to say but people with chronic illness have closed down on life." He crunched on a raw carrot.

"So you think I don't want to live enough, that's why I'm ill?" Adelaide could hardly believe anyone, much less a friend, could be so cruel.

"Through Kabbalah, I've met some fantastic people, they're so high on life they never get sick. Believe me Ade, not even a cold."

Adelaide couldn't speak.

"Until we're on their spiritual level there'll always be hospitals and treatments for the rest of us. I'd better get back, Donna's in a mood today." He snapped his lunchbox closed and left the room. Adelaide felt winded. Donna entered the staff room.

"It's been a hell of a morning." She plopped a tea bag into a mug and flicked on the kettle. She turned to Adelaide. Adelaide tried to smile. "Are you crying? Again."

"I'm sorry, it was Bret …" Donna stopped her.

"Listen, Ade, you have to decide if you can cope at work. If you can't hold it together, then you need to think about leaving."

So she left. Everything had changed and pretending it hadn't, that everything was normal, that she was just like Bret (only on a lower plane of existence) was not possible, not on any level.

The library was quiet, which was normal for the mid-afternoon slump. Donna was at the desk, tidying up, attempting to look busy. One of the assistants was reshelving books; she couldn't see who it was but could hear the muffled sound of books being shuffled and inserted on the shelf. Walking amongst the aisles she inhaled the smell and ran her hand over the rows of books. She loved the library; it had been a safe place.

Bret's voice carried across the room.

"Come on, ladies. Welcome. Sit down." The snug was set amongst the main fiction section and she could just see Bret sitting on one of the comfy chairs within a closed circle. It was the book club. Adelaide wondered if Bret was the regular group leader now. For a brief moment she experienced a surge of jealousy. Sitting in an empty chair, she decided she would join the group. She didn't have anything better to do.

At five past the hour, Bret began. "So, ladies …" A dapper chap cleared his throat. Bret laughed. "And of course, gentleman." The women giggled. It was obvious Bret was good at this. People loved him and she had too—except for his clutching at a merry-go-round of spiritual beliefs. The book club had been her responsibility and she was ashamed to admit to herself that she'd made sure of it. Bret wouldn't have had a chance when she was alive.

Adelaide had worked out that when in the land of the living she was trapped wherever she arrived. She had no control over where the open door sent her. Going through an exterior door led her back to her family house; it was a closed cycle. She longed to see Simon, but would have to wait until the door led her to him. After the book club, she couldn't bear to leave. Even if no one could hear or see her it was revitalising for her to be around people. Deciding to stay until closing time, she followed Bret on his duties. It would be just like being at work. Chattering on, she talked at Bret, recounting shared experiences or telling him about her new life, trying to make sense of it.

"I don't even know how it's decided where I go when I walk through the front door. Why am I at the library today but not yesterday? I'm just here. Isn't that crazy?" By the end of the day, she was fed up with talking to herself.

The dusk was beautiful. One of the features of the library that made it so special was its combination of old stone and glass. From the main desk the local park could be seen, and the evening light reflected gold into the building.

"The library will be closing in fifteen minutes. Please check out your books at the front desk in the next five minutes." Donna loved making announcements. As the last users left the building Bret stood near to Donna, hovering. "Go on then, get lost."

He grabbed his coat and bag from behind the service desk and was gone within thirty seconds, waving as he went. Adelaide wished she could go with him.

It had been important to Adelaide to know her life meant something to Simon and Imogen, as if love was a consolation. She kept asking them, "Do you love me?", "Will you miss me when I'm gone?". "You won't forget me, will you?" If she was loved then her life hadn't been wasted. Imogen was matter-of-fact.

"Of course I love you, don't be silly."

All the time, Simon told her he loved her but wouldn't entertain talk of a time when Adelaide would be gone.

"No one is dying today or tomorrow. I'm not thinking beyond that. Let's just keep going and in thirty years we'll look back having spent a lifetime together." It infuriated and comforted her in equal measures. She needed him to be realistic about their situation to express her grief, but his denial blocked her. However, his talent to compartmentalize helped her to contain her sadness and live in the moment. And that was a small gift. Having so few moments left, she was trying not to squander them on grief and anger. When she told him this, she joked she'd have time for that when she dead.

Three weeks after the diagnosis was finally confirmed, Imogen went into labour. Adelaide stood at the bottom of the bed peering over Imogen's raised feet. She'd been having contractions for some hours, with little progress, but Adelaide and Jack had refused to leave. The nurse warned them it could be a long wait but they still insisted. When the time came to actually push, Adelaide was scared for Imogen. Childbirth was dangerous. There were no guarantees it would end happily. She wanted the baby but her priority was Imogen.

"The epidural isn't working, it hurts." Imogen raised her voice.

"It's okay, you're doing fine. Just keep calm ..."

Imogen shouted. "For fuck's sake, how can I keep calm when I feel like I'm splitting open?" Jack was holding onto her hand and kissed her head. Imogen shooed him away.

"Get off. I can't breathe with you all over me."

He stepped back and looked at the midwife, searching for an explanation. The midwife smiled at him.

"It's okay, we usually hear much worse."

Adelaide stood back from the scene. Staring from Imogen to the machine that monitored the baby's heart-rate, she expected it to stop at any moment.

"Keep going, breathe, wait for the contraction, and then push." Imogen screamed.

After Imogen had been pushing for nearly three hours the midwife told her to stop.

"The baby is twisted and the shoulders are stuck. Don't worry, the baby's heart rate is fine, it's not in distress, but I am going to ask the paediatrician to help. If you agree."

"I don't have much choice." Imogen was exhausted. The midwife spoke to her trainee.

"Can you go and tell Sister that we need Dr. Patel's assistance in Suite 5. Thanks, Gem."

Adelaide panicked. Imogen had had her legs in the air for hours and the baby was stuck. She understood now why bringing life into the world was so dangerous. The midwife remained calm. "I'll show you." She pushed her hands into Imogen's vagina and pulled it apart to reveal the dark hairy head of the baby. Jack smiled. "You've certainly got a hairy one," the midwife laughed.

Adelaide was overwhelmed: simultaneously disturbed and amazed. It was incredible how the vagina changed and mutated to provide the appropriate canal for the birth. The human body was amazing—except hers. Hers had turned against her. It had given up without her permission.

Within minutes of the paediatrician being in the room, she had decided Imogen would have to go to theatre. And within another few minutes Imogen had been wheeled away, Jack following in gown and gloves. Adelaide waited alone in the delivery suite. Steeped in worries of what could go wrong, she watched the clock and stepped through what she imagined was happening in the operating theatre. The baby was twisted; maybe forceps would be used to tease it out, or the ventouse would drag the baby into the world—instruments and techniques seemingly designed for medieval torture. If Imogen or the baby became distressed there would have to be an emergency C-section. Adelaide couldn't help her thoughts sliding into disaster. Jack might come back holding a baby but crying, explaining that Imogen hadn't made it. Half an hour had passed and Adelaide was frantic. She was sure either one or both of them were dead.

The midwife wheeled in a transparent cot and parked it next to her.

"Imogen—is she alright?" Adelaide was exhausted with nerves.

"No need to look so worried, she's in the recovery room. They'll bring her through in a little while. Aren't you interested in your baby niece?" Adelaide looked into the cot. "I'll leave you two together."

The midwife left the room and Adelaide was alone with the baby. Wrapped tight in a blanket, her eyes closed, she was perfect, with her wrinkled, red face. To Adelaide, she looked like a tiny pixie on loan from the spirit world. She wanted to stroke her face, but refrained for fear of harming her or infecting her with human concerns.

"Hello, little baby," she said, and the baby opened her eyes. Adelaide was ecstatic; the baby could hear her. They were aware of one another. In that instant, Adelaide fell in love with her sister's baby. Immediately and without conditions and in every way, until the end of time.

Then Adelaide remembered she'd never see her grow up. The baby would never know her.

"My baby has a baby. Let me see her."

Imogen handed her baby over to their mother.

"She is adorable. Well done, sweetheart." Their mother

stared down, grinning at the child, and their father peered over her shoulder.

"She looks just like me."

"No, she doesn't look like a gnarly old gargoyle like you." They both laughed. Her father came over and kissed Adelaide on the cheek and gave her an encouraging squeeze on the arm. He'd never kissed her before her diagnosis. This was his way of communicating his support. They never spoke about it, but she sometimes caught him staring at her with a sad, hangdog expression. It almost made her feel sorry for him. But since the baby had been born a day ago, her fury had increased. Her parents were both in their mid-sixties; they'd lived a good life. Looking around the ward, she watched doting grandparents. Some were sprightly and smart, active if grey-haired; others shuffled up the ward, unable to move without help. She belonged to the latter group, only thirty-five years too early. Jealous of pensioners, she raged against the loss of her old age. "Hexed" was the word that came to her. What terrible thing had she done to deserve being damned in such a way?

All of the ghost stories she'd read had been wrong. There seemed no way to make people see you when you were dead. Adelaide waited outside Simon's workplace, staring up at the building. A routine when alive, every Tuesday night she'd meet him from work and they'd go for a meal together as a treat to break up the working week. Tuesdays had been her short day. But now, Adelaide couldn't go into the building; walking over the threshold would take her back to her family house. Replicating her past habit, she waved at Simon through the office's plate glass window. Only this time, he didn't hold up his hand to indicate he'd be five minutes. It still gave her pleasure to watch him as he packed his things away for the day, his movements familiar and dear. She kept waiting for him to lift his head and search for her as he had in the past. But he was oblivious to her presence. She was invisible.

Keeping up with Simon's pace was tricky; he was tall and had a long stride. To her advantage she was able to dart through the crowd, creating her own pathway. Desperate not to lose sight of him, she broke into a partial run. It was cruel she'd been dumped in the street. As soon as he went into a building, her way would be blocked; locked as she was in her cycle of purgatory. When Simon turned each corner she imagined holding his hand, and running slightly to keep up with him as she had so many times before. They'd chat about their day and choose what they wanted to eat, their conversation full of the excitement of having completed a day's work and looking forward to the evening ahead. As he entered the pub she stopped and watched him through the glass wall. His back was resolutely to her, standing stiff and unbending at the bar. He looked grimly alone, as if he was suffering from an invisible disease of his own. And she couldn't comfort him. She couldn't even go to him. She prayed for him to get a window seat. A light rain drizzled, creating a grey mist, which hung over the river. Haunting wasn't as she'd thought it would be, not at all.

She wasn't scared of dying, she just wanted more life. The only thing that terrified her was the idea of her dead body being alone in the mortuary. Being locked into a stainless steel cell seemed so lonely. Her body was gradually weakening and as time passed she would notice, almost by accident, with a casualness that belied her emotions, something she could no longer do: bending down; picking something up; removing a jar lid. It was the small inconveniences that catalogued her decline.

The first time she couldn't get up from the sofa was alarming. Adelaide sat watching Elinor play. Sitting on the floor, surrounded by toys, she grabbed at a small blue elephant just beyond her grasp. It gave Adelaide pleasure to watch her and she couldn't help grinning. Elinor's expression was one of intense concentration as she focused on the elephant. Her small, plump fingers touched the edge of an ear. Unable to grasp it, she pushed forward a little harder until she rocked onto all fours.

"Imogen, come and see. I think Nell is going to crawl." Adelaide shouted. No response. Adelaide tried to stand, using her usual method of placing her hands on the sofa either side of her hips and rocking forward. She couldn't get the momentum she needed to stand. She rested and tried again; she failed.

This was a pattern she came to recognise. She would learn to live with her various disabilities and cope well. It was okay. And then something would change without her having realised it. Halfway to the bus stop she couldn't go on, her legs were heavy and she shuffled, unable to lift her feet high enough to clear the ground.

"Are you sure? Can't you try?" Simon urged her.

"I am trying, what do you think I'm doing? I need the wheelchair." She hobbled towards a wall and rested against it. "I'll wait here."

"But you were walking before." Simon was exasperated.

"Now I'm not. Please Simon. It's hard enough without an argument."

Before she became ill, the idea of being a wheelchair user would have been abhorrent to Adelaide, but now it was a relief. Putting it off, she struggled to walk, convincing herself she was coping just fine. She hadn't fully understood that it was there to help her live as normally as possible, and because she waited until it was out of dire necessity, the transition was a little easier.

Her relief, however, was followed by an inevitable period of adjustment. People stared. She was young; she must be a curiosity. People carried the same look; at first puzzled and then embarrassed as they lowered their eyes. This never varied, whether the individual was young or old, male or female.

Being pushed around was frustrating and sometimes frightening. In the first few days she nearly rolled into the road when Simon stopped to put on his gloves. Turned out there was a reason they'd been told to apply the brakes whenever the wheelchair was stationary. And there were times when Simon overshot and knocked her feet into shop shelving or against doorways. Or when she wanted to look at something specific in a shop she had to explain, "There, no, over there, in front of the birthday cards, there." It was freezing in the chair; even a slight breeze was uncomfortable. Returning from outings in the middle of winter, it would take her hours to warm up and she'd snuggle against Simon until each part of her reached normal body temperature. Her feet rarely did.

Any trip out of the house was a faff. Adelaide needed help with everything. Washing, dressing, putting on her coat, hat and gloves. She still hadn't given up the need to look good and had persuaded Simon, much to his horror, to blow-dry her hair. The result was surprisingly good. Although it wasn't how she would have done it herself, she didn't want to be ungrateful or dissuade him, so tactfully accepted the result. If she was very careful she could still apply makeup. It was slow and not as precise as she'd previously been able to do but she was adamant that even as a curiosity in a wheelchair she could retain some sartorial standards. But everything was a compromise.

When using the bus for the first time, both Adelaide and Simon were shocked. They were off to Elinor's first birthday party. Simon pushed the button for disabled access. An alarm sounded inside the bus. They waited. Everyone else mooched onto the bus and took their seats. Another alarm went off and the doors shut in front of them. The alarm continued beeping. A ramp slowly emerged from the bottom of the door. The doors reopened.

"The wheelchair area is required, please clear the area. The wheelchair area is required, please clear the area."

A young mother with a buggy parked in the wheelchair section began to fold it up. She avoided looking at them.

People shuffled down the gangway, attempting to make room. Simon pushed Adelaide into the bus and everyone watched them as he struggled to manoeuvre the chair into the restricted area. A yellow pole blocked the way and Simon had to jerk her into position to get her back against the padded rest. Adelaide cringed. She had become the centre of attention for all the wrong reasons.

Being independent, able-bodied and healthy had meant that she'd lived half-hidden, taking up as little of life as possible. Increasingly dependent, she was being forced into full sight.

"It's Auntie Adelaide and Uncle Simon." Imogen held the door open and standing behind her was Elinor, who was holding onto a wooden walker.

"Happy birthday, sweetie. I can't believe she's so confident on her feet." Adelaide laughed at the tiny girl, standing defiant.

"Yes, she can walk really well with the baby-walker." Imogen stroked her small, chestnut head. "Jack, come and help Simon get Ade in please." They lifted her wheelchair over the threshold and Simon pushed her through the house to the back garden. The barbeque smelled delicious and, behind the smoke rising from the coals, her dad raised a kitchen utensil in greeting. Her mum got up from her chair and limped towards her. She bent down and gave her a kiss on the cheek.

"Hello, darling, I've been in the wars, as you can see." She indicated her bandaged foot. This was typical of her

mentally impaired too.

Adelaide pushed the button to let the driver know she wanted to get off. She couldn't hear the alarm so pushed it again: still there was no sound. Simon was sitting a few rows back and she signalled to him. He shook his head, trying to let her know he didn't understand what she was trying to say. The bus stopped and let passengers off, the doors closed again and the bus started to pull away.

"You've got to press the special button, love," an old woman instructed her. Then an old man next to her started to shout.

"Driver! Driver! Stop! Stop the bus! There's a woman in a wheelchair that wants off!" Simon fought his way towards her.

"Driver! Stop!" the old man continued. At last the bus stopped and the alarm began. Simon managed to get to her.

"Release your brakes." Adelaide took her brakes off and the chair rolled forward into the old woman before Simon had a chance to grab it.

"Simon!" He clasped the chair. "I'm so sorry," Adelaide apologised.

"Don't worry, love." The old woman patted her leg with sympathy. The bus was too packed to let them get out easily. The alarm beeped and the doors drew back. A dozen of the theatre students traipsed off the bus and stood either side of the ramp as if a welcoming committee. Simon wheeled her down the ramp past the students.

"Well, that's the bus then," she said over her shoulder, making a face at Simon, who shared her mocking grin.

Bret had been right after all. When alive, she hadn't lived fully enough, taken all the opportunities she could have. She'd had her share of life, been found wanting, and so the rest was denied her. The million things she hadn't done haunted her: international travel, adventure, having a baby, her dream of working at the British Library, friends she should have bothered to maintain contact with, those hobbies she'd always intended to pick up. She had let it all slip by.

Not really knowing whom she was addressing, she admitted to some unseen force that she now knew she'd done it wrong, and now she was good, she had changed, she understood what was required of her and could do it better, if she was given the chance to try. She promised.

Adelaide stood on the threshold of the patio door watching her family. Her mother was playing a game of Frisbee with Elinor. Missing the Frisbee, Elinor chased after it as it travelled across the grass. She pretended to trip and . rolled behind it, laughing.

"That's enough, darling. Nanny's too hot."

Jack laughed at Elinor's dramatic reaction. "She'll make a great footballer, taking a dive like that." Jack kicked a ball in Elinor's direction. Running after it, she pulled back her small foot and kicked it. It rolled less than a metre. She ran after it again. Adelaide wanted to call to Elinor and join in with the game. As usual, Adelaide's father stood behind the barbeque.

"Two minutes on these burgers." He was poking a patty, squeezing the fat onto the coals. It sizzled. "Delicious." He was pleased with the result.

Imogen walked up behind her, carrying a large bowl of salad, and instinctively Adelaide moved out of her way. Putting the salad on the table, turning, Imogen smiled.

"Listen. Mum, Dad, I'm pregnant." She laughed.

"Oh, my darling, that's wonderful news." Their mother rushed forward, kissed and then hugged her. Imogen was delighted. Adelaide felt sick. Only a few months since she'd died and they didn't seem to care she'd gone at all. Adelaide couldn't watch anymore and stepped over the threshold.

Being dead was complicated. She could move, sort of enjoy day-to-day living, and visit the living world. But she was disconnected from it. Her darling sister was having another baby and didn't appear to show any signs of missing her. Haunting came with too many unexplained restrictions. There were rules she didn't understand and no one to explain them to her. She had no control over where she would end up in the living world; she wanted to see Simon, but the front door rarely delivered her to him. The days passed in a bland routine: getting up, doing a few exercises, reading, watching a film—a repeat—snoozing, having dinner and then more TV. Often, she'd wake up on the sofa having fallen asleep during the evening. Each day was identical to the next. She had no idea when the door would open or where it would lead her.

As usual, she sat on the sofa eating her dinner. Hot dogs again. She put the plate down next to her. There were only so many hot dogs one person could stomach.

"Fancy some hot dog, Hector?" The cat barely twitched. If she could get someone to talk to her, that would make all the difference. It wasn't food that made you alive, it was other people. "What do you think, Hector? Maybe, I could try saying 'BOO!' to people or moving things around like ghosts are supposed to do?" Hector opened his eyes for a moment and then continued snoozing. It was no surprise fictional ghosts were often angry if haunting was so miserable.

When Elinor was out of the house, Adelaide waited for her to return. There were those special days when Elinor would come straight to her, climb on the bed and give her a kiss. Occasionally, when Adelaide had the breath, she read to her. Elinor held the book and turned the pages. They laughed at animal noises, but now Elinor would tell her she was doing it wrong and demonstrate her superior interpretation. When Adelaide couldn't read, her breath shallow and restricted, Imogen would come and sit on the bed and read to them both, Elinor snuggling next to Adelaide, and Adelaide dozing, curled around her niece.

Over the months she'd become tired of being lifted, transferred from bed to wheelchair to commode. Her body ached and she lived in fear of being dropped. It was hard for others to fully understand that, if she fell, it hurt her so much more: her limbs would twist and become trapped under the weight of her immobile body. It was excruciating. Eventually, a hoist was introduced and she barely left her bed. The frustration of being static was one she'd learned to temper. Being left with something just out of reach, or freezing with the window open, or sweating when it was closed, were regular occurrences.

—◈—

Archie was a beautiful baby, plump and content. Observing his sleeping face was calming. Adelaide sat next to Imogen, smiling to herself as she watched them. Elinor was crouched on the floor sorting the pieces of a jigsaw puzzle.

"Find the edges first, darling," Imogen suggested. She was tired and her hair needed a wash.

"Like this, Mummy?" Elinor held up a piece for Imogen's inspection.

"Does that look like it has a straight side?"

Elinor stared at it and giggled. "It's all wiggly." Elinor was holding up pieces one after another, all with wiggly edges.

"No, that one." Imogen was pointing to an appropriate piece, but Elinor kept picking others.

"Next to it, to the left," Imogen snapped. "No, the left, not the right." Adelaide knelt down beside Elinor and handed her the piece. She hadn't really been meaning to pick something up, but she did. And it was so easy. A wide smile spread across Adelaide's face. But the child took it without reaction.

"This one, Mummy?"

"Yes, at last. Now find the rest." Imogen hadn't noticed.

212

Adelaide continued pushing pieces of the puzzle towards Elinor and they worked together in unacknowledged silence. It only took them a few minutes to assemble the edges of the puzzle. Imogen looked up from Archie. "Wow, Nell—that was quick."

Elinor nodded and smiled, half glancing towards Adelaide. Adelaide wanted to grab her to see if the child really could see her. It did seem as if she was looking at her, but she couldn't be sure.

"Time for bed now, you can finish the rest tomorrow."

Adelaide lay on the sofa and watched the trees being blown by the wind. Lurching shadows reflected against the living room walls. She'd decided not to go back to her halfway house. There was no guarantee when she'd be able to return to the living world and she had to know if Elinor had seen her. She didn't want to scare either Elinor or Imogen but there must be a way of communicating without causing alarm. Her fantasy was all three of them chatting together, sharing a life again. Excitement made her involuntarily stand; it might be possible to have a new kind of life.

Running up the stairs, exhilaration still carried her forward. On the landing she slowed and crept towards Imogen's bedroom. The door was open. Adelaide stood at the threshold and watched Imogen and Jack sleeping. Jack was on his back, mouth open, snoring, and Imogen snuggled next to him, curled into a foetal position. Her clenched fists nestled under her chin. She looked cute.

Adelaide edged towards the baby's basket. Archie was wriggling his arms and legs as if fighting an imaginary foe. He squeaked and thrashed his head. His mouth opened in prelude to a cry. Imogen stirred. Adelaide withdrew.

A hump of duvet had collected at the head of the bed. A small foot stuck out from the bottom and a mass of hazel hair from the top. The room was beautiful. The shelves were full of books and soft, plush animals, wooden toys and games. Just how she imagined a child's bedroom should be. Cartoon woodland creatures and toadstools covered the soft furnishings. Above the bed hovered large paper orbs in deep pink, bright orange and blue. Adelaide hadn't been upstairs in her sister's house for years. Imogen had consulted her on colours and fabric but once she'd lost her ability to climb stairs she'd been unable to see the final result. Imogen had done a good job. There was a child-sized armchair, again covered with cute fungi. Adelaide would have loved it herself as a child. She pulled it alongside the bed and sat down. Her knees made extreme triangle shapes. Leaning forward she coaxed the duvet away from Elinor's face. The child wriggled. Adelaide froze, but Elinor continued to sleep, her face now peeping out of the duvet. Picking up a book, she opened it, expecting the pages to be bare. But the words were there on the page. The relief of seeing the text felt like breathing new life. So in the living world she could experience new things: it was possible to live again. She began to read, whispering the words.

"Come on, missus, time to get up." Imogen pulled back the bedroom curtains and the light hurt Adelaide's eyes. From the way Elinor hid under the duvet, she was sure the abrupt awakening had been a shock to her too. The book she'd been reading had slipped to the floor. Her neck hurt and was stiff from having hung forward on her chest as she'd slept in the tiny chair.

"Time to get out of bed. School this morning." Elinor sat up. Her hair was matted and she rubbed her eyes. She reminded Adelaide of the pixie she'd seen at birth.

"Red or yellow?" Imogen held up a red cord dress and a pair of yellow, heavy-cotton dungarees. Elinor shook her head.

"No, I want the green one." Elinor was sulking.

"It's in the wash. We'll go with the red." Stamping her feet on the mattress, Elinor cried.

"Not this morning, Elinor, I'm not in the mood." Picking knickers, vest and tights from the draw, Imogen assembled the outfit. This wasn't how Adelaide would wake Elinor. She'd do it gently and give her time. Imogen was being too harsh.

"Now, madam." Elinor slid from the bed and crossed the room. "Arms up." Imogen pulled the pajama top over Elinor's head and replaced it with a vest.

"Can I have a story?" Elinor asked.

"I don't have time, sweet pea, I've still got to get the baby ready."

Elinor thought for a moment and then said, "What about the lady?" Adelaide couldn't believe it.

"Lady? What do you mean, sweetie? Left foot, please."

Imogen wriggled Elinor's foot into the tights.

"The lady that read me a story last night." Elinor held out her right foot.

"Stand up." Imogen pulled up the tights. "You mean Mummy read you a story."

Elinor shook her head. "No, the lady." Elinor's insistence frightened Imogen.

"You're just being silly and playing with Mummy. Come downstairs and get some breakfast." She led Elinor from the room.

Elinor could hear Adelaide. She couldn't leave them now.

Adelaide waited for Imogen to leave Elinor's bedroom. A night-light illuminated the far side of the room and Elinor was snuggled up to her neck under the duvet. As Adelaide walked across the room, Elinor sat up, listening. Adelaide selected the book from the previous evening. Elinor watched.

"Not that one." Elinor hopped from her bed and ran to the shelf and pulled down a book. She laid it in front of her chair and got back into bed. Adelaide was overwhelmed. Picking up the book, she began to read. Elinor listened, seemingly unconcerned by the strangeness of the situation.

"Can you see all the animals?" Adelaide held the book up. "You used to love the camels. They look so grumpy." Elinor nodded, giggling.

"They're silly." She couldn't stop giggling. Adelaide emulated the camel's expression in the way she would have done when alive. "You look silly too." Adelaide's camel face faded.

"You can see me?" Elinor looked at her and nodded.

"What are you doing still awake?" Imogen stood in the doorway.

"Having a story."

"Well, you should be asleep. You're being too noisy—you'll wake the baby." She bent down and covered Elinor with the duvet and kissed her on the head.

"It's not just me." Elinor sat up again.

"Don't be silly, Nell. Lie down." Elinor refused, stiffening her back in protest.

"It's the lady, she's silly too."

Imogen stood back. "I don't like this, Nell. There's no lady. It's just your imagination." She forced the child down again. "Now, please go to sleep."

Adelaide watched them. She wanted to reassure Imogen it was okay. To wave the book around in her face would be too shocking. Adelaide glanced around the room, looking for a solution. There were some wooden letters on the shelf. She arranged them to spell "Ade". Elinor shouted, pointing.

"Look!" Imogen stared at the letters for a long time. She surveyed the room as if expecting to find someone standing behind her and then turned to Elinor and shouted.

"I've had enough of this! Now get to sleep." She almost ran from the room. Maybe the reason people couldn't see Adelaide was because they couldn't imagine it was possible. Imogen wasn't yet able to believe in her.

Sitting at the piano, Adelaide scrutinised the photograph. Their cousin's wedding had been fun. She'd always had the best of times with Imogen. Although Imogen couldn't see her yet, Adelaide knew it was possible. The house was quiet. Imogen had taken Elinor to reception class and Jack was at work. Placing her fingers on the piano keys, she let them rest. It had been a long time since she'd played. Pressing the keys down, she enjoyed the sound. Running her fingers along the keys, she played a scale and then another and another. It was exhilarating. Sorting through the music books on the rest, she found *Old Time Rags*. She'd loved playing rags. They were joyful and they'd often cheered her up. "Chipmunk Rag" was simple and one of her earliest pieces. At first she tried the right hand, playing slowly to make sure of getting every note correct. Playing it over until it was natural under her fingers. She did the same for the left. Initially, when she put her hands together, her playing was faltering but soon, as her confidence grew, so did the speed. Playing was liberating. If she could make Imogen see her, she would have a life. The three of them could be happy. She wouldn't be able to leave the house at first but in time she might be able to control where she went. Maybe she'd be able to go on dinner dates with Simon. They could be a couple again, even lovers. For now, she'd focus on her life here. But in the future, she would find a way to see Simon too.

The piano lid slammed shut. Imogen collected up the music in her arms and locked the piano lid. Adelaide was shocked; she hadn't even heard Imogen enter the room.

She followed as Imogen hurried away.

"Imogen, it's me, Ade." Imogen gave no indication she could hear her. But she had heard the piano. This was proof. Adelaide was elated; now she just had to get her to see and talk to her. Imogen was scared and would need coaxing and encouragement: it was an unusual situation for all of them. But now there was real hope.

"Did you write this?" Imogen held a note up at Jack's duvet-clad body. He was still asleep. Imogen shook his shoulder and he rolled, groaning as he emerged from sleep.

"What!?" Groggy, he sat up as she waved the piece of paper in his face. He grabbed it from her. It read, "I love you. Ade." She didn't allow him to answer.

"And this." She threw the picture of Imogen and Adelaide, which usually sat on top of the piano, in his lap. "Did you put this by the bed?"

Leaning against the windowsill, Adelaide was watching. She wondered why Imogen would think Jack had put them there.

"As a joke. Did you do it as a joke?" Adelaide thought it wouldn't have been a particularly funny joke.

"Why on earth would I do that? It wouldn't be a very funny joke." Adelaide nodded in agreement.

"I don't know." Covering her face, Imogen cried. "But what the hell were they doing there?"

"Sweetie, calm down. Maybe Nell put the photo there because she knows how much you miss Ade." He put his arms around her but she wriggled free.

"What about the note? Did she write that?" Screwing up the note, she threw it on the floor.

"No, I guess not. It's probably an old one she found in a drawer," he offered. Imogen was silent for a moment, thinking.

"Do you think Nell remembers Ade very well?"

"I guess so, it hasn't been that long and they were close. Why?"

"She's been saying and doing some weird things lately. Talking about a lady reading her a story, and she spelled 'Ade' with her bricks. I've just tried to move on and keep things normal, so the kids don't grow up in a sad house. Maybe I should talk about Ade more, but I can't. It's too hard."

"I don't think you should make a big deal of it. If she does anything else, ignore it. She'll soon forget. Kids do."

This wasn't what Adelaide had expected. Imogen didn't need to live in a sad house cleansed of her memory. Adelaide would have to make her understand they could be happy together again.

As teenagers, hiding one of her sister's shoes was one of the tactics Adelaide had employed if she didn't want Imogen to come out with her, and one Imogen had used when she didn't want Adelaide to go out without her. With only two years difference between their ages, their social circles had overlapped. Or more exactly, Imogen had infiltrated Adelaide's. Their parents joked that Imogen had become her shadow. At first, the disappearing shoes had been a prank both girls found funny.

Imogen was sure to understand what a missing shoe would mean. But taking away one boot of her favourite pair hadn't even been noticed. After looking for a few minutes, slightly late and a bit annoyed, she'd just worn an alternative pair. Using a black plastic sack, Adelaide took one shoe from every pair that Imogen owned and put it in the bag. She even took the posh, "going out" ones. She'd done this before. On the evening of her school leaving celebrations, Imogen, as usual, had insisted she'd come along. Adelaide didn't usually mind, but she'd wanted this occasion to be sister-free, an event special to her and her friends. Secretly, Adelaide was jealous. Imogen smoked and hung around at break times with the cool smoking gang, who congregated at the bottom of the sports field. Hilarious when drunk, Imogen drank all the more for entertainment value. She even had more experience with boys than Adelaide. Adelaide had been cast as the boring, responsible older sister, trying to keep Imogen out of trouble. Imogen was more fun and definitely less uptight. The night of the sixth-form party, Adelaide wanted to let go of her prim sensibilities and have a great night out. To make sure Imogen couldn't come along, Adelaide had collected one shoe of every pair she owned and hidden them in the loft. Imogen was furious and sulked for over a week.

Now though, Imogen was hysterical. She tore open every cupboard searching for her shoes. Jack and Elinor watched as she marched around ransacking the house. The contents of every cupboard were strewn across the floor.

"You did this!" she screamed at Jack as yet more rubbish

was ejected from its storage space.

"Why would I? Imogen, this is madness."

"I'll bet it was you." She turned on Elinor, shouting. "Get my shoes now!"

Elinor began to cry. Imogen was out of control. Adelaide had been sure Imogen would understand and laugh. To blame Elinor was ridiculous. Pushing the bag from the top of the stairs, Adelaide watched from the landing as it flopped down over each step. Imogen, Jack and Nell gathered around it. Jack shook his head at Imogen.

"I thought we'd agreed to underplay this. I'm taking Nell out for an ice cream and giving you a chance to tidy up."

It was becoming obvious to Adelaide that Imogen was closed to her. Willfully obtuse, she suspected. Rejected and frustrated, the new life she'd dreamed of was slipping away. Imogen was a coward: she didn't want to find out if a new life was even possible for them.

Adelaide wouldn't be ignored.

It was Adelaide's turn to be Imogen's shadow. When Imogen tidied up, Adelaide followed—untidying. As Imogen replaced Elinor's books and toys, Adelaide rearranged them. If the oven was on low, she turned it up to its highest setting. At night, she'd rearrange items of furniture to suit her own preference. Carefully removing the contents of the airing cupboard, she laid them out in the hallway. The house keys were removed from Imogen's bag and placed in her coat pocket, and the car keys removed from their hook and left in a bowl in the dining room. But Imogen could have been a robot. She continued going about the daily duties she had been programmed to perform, ignoring the damage caused and starting over again.

Slowly but surely, with every correction the robot made, Adelaide became enraged.

Archie's tiny hands were clenched into fists and his arms were extended above his head. He was at peace. As Adelaide watched him sleep, she envied his lack of self-awareness; his body rose and fell with each breath. Regular in his feeding routine, Adelaide knew he'd wake up soon. Imogen was hugging Jack from behind and, sleeping side by side, they looked like the perfect adoring couple. Adelaide wondered how long Jack would remain oblivious to her struggle with Imogen. Wriggling in his cot, Archie began to wake up. A feeble squeak turned into a loud cry. Imogen opened her eyes and lay motionless for a moment. Crying, without even taking a breath, Archie's arms and legs were taut and still, suspended by his fury.

"Okay, sweetheart, Mummy's coming." Imogen sat up and swung her legs onto the floor. Again, she sat for a minute, rubbing her eyes. Adelaide stood observing her from just a few feet away. As Imogen walked to the cot, Adelaide stepped back to let her pass. Imogen lifted Archie from the cot and turned back towards the bed. As she did, Adelaide extended her foot. Imogen fell forward. Hard. And as she went down, her head clipped the edge of the bedside cabinet. Archie screamed as he hit the floor. Clamping her hand to her mouth, Adelaide recoiled with shock. She hadn't meant for Imogen or the baby to get hurt.

But then, as Adelaide thought about it, maybe this was what was needed to get her attention.

"We're all going on a summer holiday, no more working for a week or two." Imogen was singing at Elinor who was struggling to pull a rucksack onto her back. She had a pair of sunglasses perched on her head.

"Holiday, hooray!" Elinor clapped. "Mummy, how long?"

"Daddy is just packing the car and then we'll be off."

"Hooray!" Elinor spun around. Adelaide was sitting at the dining room table watching the hustle of the holiday preparations. Imogen was taking Elinor away. Adelaide was being punished.

"Okay, that's the boot done. Anything else, Imogen?"

"Just the kids. Thanks for this, Jack." She kissed him on the cheek.

"If my lady needs a holiday, then that's what she shall have. I know it's been tough with Archie and Ade." Imogen turned away to see Elinor spinning round and round.

"Stop that, Nell, you'll be sick." Ignoring her mother, Elinor continued spinning. Archie was in his bouncy chair on the floor and she stumbled, landing on top of him.

"I told you to stop and now look what you've done." She dragged Elinor from the baby and held her by the arm. "Can you do nothing you're told?" Her spittle sprayed on

Elinor's face. Adelaide was on her feet, ready to rescue the child, but Jack stepped in.

"Off to the toilet, you." He gently ushered her to the door. Archie was screaming. Imogen lifted him out of his chair and held him to her shoulder.

"It's okay, you're okay," she repeated as she paced the room. Adelaide watched Imogen with Archie; she looked content with him, but with Elinor she was short-tempered and resentful. It was wrong for Imogen to treat her children in such different ways. Imogen was not the mother Adelaide had thought she would be. Or the mother that Adelaide herself would have been. If the option hadn't been stolen from her.

"We're all going on a summer holiday." Jack was singing as he danced into the room with Elinor in his arms. "Come on, let's get going."

"I'll just get the baby's things. You get Elinor sorted."

"Aye, aye, capt'n." Jack swept Elinor out of the door. Imogen laid the baby in his chair and checked through his bag. She added a packet of wipes, picked up the baby and left the house. Adelaide had been abandoned. Again.

The first thing Adelaide did was to make a replica of the calendar. They would only be gone for ten days, but to cross off each day as it passed would remind her that her solitary confinement was temporary. She was alone but at least she could look forward to Elinor's return.

Imogen used to say that she loved Ade, that she couldn't bear to lose her. But now that they'd been given a chance to be together again she was ignoring her. It had been

225

naive to think that Imogen had ever really cared about her. To think that Imogen was turning away made Adelaide sad, angry and confused. The certainties her security was built on were unravelling. Like finally admitting she was jealous of Imogen's social skills, she now conceded she'd tricked herself into believing they loved each other equally. It was obvious. Imogen had always been a selfish brat. She had only wanted Ade for her friends. Wearing Ade's brand new clothes and sneaking her coat over them before Adelaide could see, and then revealing them to her friends and getting all the credit. New lipsticks were mutilated and eye shadows gouged from their packaging. Their relationship was only good because Adelaide had invariably let Imogen have her own way.

And Imogen knew that Elinor had been a joy to her when she was dying. Her laughter had kept her sane. Now Imogen was keeping them apart. Adelaide was perplexed at how Imogen could be so cruel.

Sun shone through the windows making the interior of the house feel dark. Longing to go outside, in compensation she opened all the windows as far as they would stretch and stood in the middle of the living room holding out her arms, relishing the cool breeze that blew throughout the house. She would at least enjoy being in the living world where she could do almost whatever she liked.
Imogen was predictable. Adelaide opened the lid to her jewellery box and there was the key to the piano. The music had just been dumped on the ottoman. Each

morning she crossed the day off her makeshift calendar and then played the piano. In the afternoon she read a new book. Imogen didn't have a very good collection and loved detective fiction. Adelaide wouldn't have read this kind of material, but now she devoured the stories of Sherlock Holmes and Hercule Poirot. At least it was new. Action films and reality TV shows, which she would have abhorred, she now enjoyed.

She was living again.

At night she slept in Elinor's bed. It made her feel close to her. The bed was a little too short, but she didn't mind curling up until she fitted in a snug ball. Keeping the night-light on, she read the titles of the books adorning the shelves. Adelaide imagined reading them with Elinor and practised the conversations they would have. They would of course point out the pictures and laugh at the jokes, but she could also help teach her to read. She'd just started school and Imogen was too busy with the baby. Adelaide could make Elinor's education a project. But there was no way she could enjoy the piano with Elinor unless Imogen accepted her.

Her anger at Imogen for taking Elinor away was flourishing. Memories from childhood popped into her head, triggered by everyday items. The carpet sweeper, which had become a family heirloom, reminded Adelaide how Imogen would do anything to get praise from their mother. Any opportunity to help out with housework was an opportunity to suck up. Their mother's request for someone to "put the carpet sweeper round" saw Imogen, within thirty seconds, dancing across the floor, pushing it back and forth in rhythmic action. On Sundays, Imogen would be up weighing ingredients in preparation for her baking session with their mother. At teatime, she'd parade into the living room, carrying a baked masterpiece oozing with fruit and cream. Their Dad would "ooh" and "ah." "Isn't she a clever clogs?" he'd say. And Ade agreed, being benevolent and good-natured; after all, cleaning and baking weren't her thing. But the truth was now obvious. Imogen had insisted on being the favourite, the only daughter who counted.

Reassessing the past led her to relive the painful split with her first boyfriend. Adelaide didn't want to think it but it was too late, the thought had already occurred. Tom was perfect as far as Adelaide was concerned. He possessed the trio of goodness: height, an athletic build and thick blonde hair, which he flicked back from his face to reveal deep-brown eyes. She was so in love.

When she'd walked in on Imogen and Tom kissing, her first thought was that he'd betrayed her. Imogen confirmed it.

"Honestly, Ade, I turned around and there he was. He didn't give me a chance to stop him." Adelaide believed her and ended the relationship. Heartbroken, Adelaide had cried every day for a term. Over the years, Imogen claimed she'd done her a favour and saved her more heartache; she'd also never have met Simon if it hadn't been for her. Adelaide had been a gullible idiot.

Each day that passed, bringing their return nearer, led

Adelaide to fantasise about how she could force Imogen to acknowledge her. She'd give it one last attempt for them all to be together—it was only reasonable—but after that she'd have to find a different solution to be with Elinor.

When Elinor came through the front door, Adelaide wanted to rush to her and hug her but Imogen was directly behind, ushering her up the hallway.

"Come on, slowcoach. Archie needs a nappy change." Elinor saw Adelaide and ran towards her.

"Heeelloooo!" She held out a colourful windmill. "Look what I've got."

Imogen stopped and stared towards where Adelaide was standing. For a moment she thought Imogen could see her.

"Hello, Imogen. I'm still waiting here. For you. For Elinor. For us."

"We're not staying here." Imogen turned and left the house. Elinor remained where she was.

"And I'm not going anywhere!" Adelaide shouted to Imogen, who was strapping Archie back in the car.

"Come and get in the car, Elinor." Imogen was standing by the driver's door. "Leave that, Jack." Jack was unpacking the boot. Bemused, he slammed it shut.

"I'll count to five, Elinor."

"No. I won't come," Elinor shouted back. She stood in the doorway.

"One." Both Imogen and Elinor stood firm. "Two." Jack walked towards Imogen.

"Not again, as soon as we get home, this is ludicrous.

Come inside and we can sort it out." Imogen turned on him.

"I don't expect you to understand. Three."

"You go and do what you need to do and I'll stay here with Nelly." He turned away and walked towards the house. Imogen got into the car and started the engine.

Elinor cried, "Mummy!" The child panicked and ran out towards the car as Imogen reversed into the road. Adelaide flung herself after her, yelling, "Wait! Nell!" and stepped out of the front door.

"Nell!" She was still running. Hector looked up from the sofa. Adelaide ran to the door and pulled on the handle. It remained closed. She shook it, crying with anger and kicking the door.

"Please open, please let me go back."

Hector was watching her with sleepy half interest. Death suited him. But then, it was a lot like his life. "What are you looking at?" Adelaide snarled at him and battled the urge to kick him across the room.

Accidents happen. And in less than a moment. Elinor might be hurt and there was no way Adelaide could find out. She was stuck in this house while her new life and Elinor were elsewhere. She couldn't keep her safe. Adelaide punched the wall in frustration. But then, it had been Imogen who put Elinor in harm's way. It was Imogen who was at fault: Imogen was an unfit mother.

The box hit the landing with force and dust billowed into the air. Opening the lid, half a dozen faces stared up at her. All the soft toys she couldn't bear to throw away, but hadn't had room for when she'd left home, had been stowed in the loft. Her favourites were Walter, a large tortoise, and Sausage Legs Fatty, a pink-faced knitted doll with stumpy arms and legs. Arranging them on her brother's bed, she thought about how she could sleep with Elinor and soothe her when she woke in the night. Adelaide would be able to devote her time to Elinor. She'd tried to reconnect with Imogen, and she'd tried hard, but now she knew how futile it was. Imogen had never loved her and then she'd tried to take Elinor away, even though she knew that the child made her life worthwhile: Imogen was a monster.

But Adelaide had worked out the solution to her problem; she just had to wait for the front door to open.

"Look at the stars, Nell, they're beautiful." Elinor stood on the ledge of the open window. She looked up into the sky as Adelaide held her around the waist. Adelaide would have to push Elinor very hard to make sure she fell with enough force to die.

"Would you like to come and stay with Auntie Adelaide?" Elinor nodded. Adelaide kissed her on the cheek. "We'll have fun and I'll take good care of you."

The light flicked on.

"You're not taking her anywhere." Imogen was standing behind them and holding out her arms. "Come to Mummy, Nell." Her voice was calm, caring and in charge. Elinor shook her head and clung onto Adelaide's neck.

Adelaide was confused. "Imogen?"

"I've been able to see you for a while. Since you took my shoes."

"But then, why …" The anger engulfed Adelaide. Imogen interrupted her.

"Because it isn't right. It isn't natural." She was as determined as Adelaide was enraged.

"We still have a chance of living together. What we've always planned. You, me and Elinor."

"It isn't living, Ade." Imogen took a step nearer.

"You don't want that? Well, I don't want you anyway. But I do want Nell." She started to peel Elinor's arms from her neck, ready to push her from the window. Imogen edged further forward.

"It's not fair, Ade, she deserves to live."

"She will be living. With me." Elinor was beginning to panic, confused by their words. She let go of Adelaide and dropped to the floor, turning towards Imogen. Catching hold of her hair, Adelaide yanked her back, securing her under her arm. Imogen continued with her implacable calmness.

"I'm so sorry you were young and you suffered, but it doesn't mean you have the right to take my child."

Adelaide hoisted Elinor onto the windowsill. The child screamed and clung to the frame, pushing back as Adelaide tried to force her through it. Imogen ran the last few steps.

"Hold on, Nelly!" Pulling Adelaide with all her strength, Imogen yanked one arm free from the child. It put Adelaide off balance and she fell backwards, dragging the child with her. Elinor screamed again, "Mummy!" and held out her arms. Imogen grabbed her. The three grappled and clung together on the floor, entangled, all fighting a grim battle. Then, with a strength that was almost superhuman, Imogen severed herself and her daughter free.

Looking down at Adelaide on the floor, Imogen was crying, her calm broken.

"Adelaide, I've missed you every day, all the time. I loved you but your time is over, you have to leave us alone. We need a normal life."

⸺❖⸺

As usual, Hector was snuggled next to Adelaide on the sofa, snoozing. She flicked through the TV channels, searching for the least unbearable repeat. Death was so unendurably boring. And it had given her plenty of opportunity to repent of her life. It was her own fault if she hadn't made the most of things before her time ran out: it had been too easy to lead a half life. Her second chance hadn't worked out either.

A familiar breeze cooled her leg. She leaned forward to look; the front door was open. Adelaide got up, crossed the room and slammed the door shut before returning to the couch. The living world was no longer her concern. But Adelaide was sure there had to be something more. And she was ready for it. Fully and completely.

SUCKING THE LIFE

It's obvious to me you're dying. Near the end. Since I've been seeing you, your voice has weakened and your breathing's shallower." Jude's arousal is palpable. If I had the strength to feel his cock it would be semi-erect. "I want to be with you until you die. The very moment. I make that commitment to you even though you've already had your eight sessions."

He's almost salivating, basking in my death. My decline, his pleasure.

"I've been to my palliative care consultant to discuss how much longer I've got."

He leans forward, eager.

"She told me that if I eat well and avoid infections, I should live quite a while."

He physically wilts. Our roles are changing; I know what he is now.

When Jude sauntered out of his office to greet us for the first time, my brother and I were both stunned by his excessive good looks. Six foot four, wide shouldered, narrow at the hip and an on-trend neatly trimmed beard adorning his chiselled chin. Nearing forty, his eyes wrinkled as he assumed a teasing smile.

Friends and family aren't over keen to talk about death. Nor are they explicit about why. When probed, the responses stay the same: "Let's just take it a day at a time" or "It won't do you any good to dwell on it." *Whack!* I'm being repeatedly smacked into silence with the tenderness of a sadist. I want to scream, "I don't want to die!" or "How can I bear what's happening!" but nobody's listening. So I'm trying out a professional. I just hadn't expected Mr. GQ.

"Hey. Pleased to meet you. I'm Jude." He held out his hand but I couldn't move, being paralysed and all. Unfazed, he slid a slender long-fingered hand into mine and gently lifted it into an inept handshake. His body was loose and he moved with ease. Ed and I chanced a furtive side-glance at one another, acknowledging our alarm at his laid-back, rainbow-rhythms demeanour. More than happy in his skin, he'd tailored his own.

"Come on through," he beckoned, gliding back to the therapy room. Ed followed, becoming flustered as he negotiated the tiny corridor and bashed the wheelchair against the doorframe in two places as we entered. He then backed out, afraid he might get analysed by just inhaling the air.

Parked opposite Jude, ensnared within his golden glow of sexuality and health, I felt like an ugly lump in a wheelchair. His abundance cruelly accentuated my lack. Raspberry ripple: cripple.

He may have to touch me. If I cried and snot rolled down my face, as it often does, he'd have to wipe it away. If I got pins and needles, he'd have to move my foot. Or remove my hat if my head got too hot—although my hair was filthy so I wouldn't be asking him to do that.

Unwilling to be scrutinised by his playful gaze, I commented on an amateurish piece of artwork, an unusually shaped cup on the desk, the lack of view from the window—anything to detract from my discomfort. Uncrossing his legs, I was sure he was more than conscious of the dynamic. Our mutual—if unacknowledged—awareness was excruciating.

"Okay. Have you had any therapy before?" He got down to business.

"None. I'm a therapy virgin."

Jesus. Why did I mention sex?

He raised his eyebrows and, as he started to speak again, bounced his head from side to side in small, contained moves.

"Well, unlike a psychologist, existential psychotherapy means I take a more philosophical approach. It's a conversation to help those who are troubled to come to terms with the limitations of existence."

I'm goal-oriented and like quantifiable success. But what was I working towards now with this existential psychotherapist? What was the worst that could happen? Death?

Awkward.

"I guess by the limitations of existence, you mean death?"

"And that we are ultimately alone without any meaning or purpose to life."

Ultimately alone; I don't want to die alone. That's what I'm doing here.

"My method helps people understand that this reality can be empowering, we can embrace our own meaning."

The meaninglessness of life has never been my problem. With thanks to the Rolling Stones, I have a workable motto: *You can't always get what you want, but if you try sometimes, you just might find you get what you need.* I'm a problem solver, I make things work, I achieve. But you can't fix anything if you're dead.

"So, on your referral form you say you want to talk explicitly about death," he prompted, placing his hands into his lap and relaxing back to listen. He was almost too relaxed, slightly slumped in his chair, his golden glow penetrating the air.

The opportunity to speak made my head dizzy with words — too many to order into any coherent sense. Grinning at him to reduce my discomfort, we sat in silence. After a pause that could be hours, I said, "I'm furious. So incredibly angry I want to smash up the whole world."

I was suddenly sobbing as I spoke. My grief, contained by the jovial support of others, had been unleashed. Salty snot streamed over my lips and into my mouth. "If I had the strength," I added. Hysterical, I alternated between laughing and crying. "There's nothing that can be done to make this better."

"Humans can't deal with limitations, but being human means working within limitations." An understatement if ever there was one. Leaning forward, he continued, "It's the limitations that frame life." I expected him to add 'man'.

"It's so unbelievably isolating, like being adrift in a small rowboat. You can see everyone on the beach but you can't get to them. They are all smiling and saying 'you're doing very well,' and nobody wants to be reminded of the horror, but it's impossible to escape."

"You've been talking in the second person. It's not abstract; it's your death. Own it."

"Man," I mentally added to the end of his sentence before trying again.

"It's not unreasonable to want to talk about my death. I'm alone. I'm only forty-five, I'm going to die and I'm devastated. I'm not ready to die. I want to scream and shout and cry. I want to show Tom and my family that it's okay to be angry, but it's too alarming and scary for them. And I'm jealous of them: they'll be grieving but at least they're going to be alive to be bloody sad. Lucky fuckers."

"You've got me now. I'm not afraid of the dying," he said, leaning forward, closing the space between us. Uneasy but not knowing why, I was unsure of how to respond. I decided to ignore it and continued.

"I just want to be able to say, 'I'm afraid I'm going to lose my voice', 'I wonder how long I've got left' and 'I wonder what my funeral will be like'. The moment any sentence has left my lips Tom shuts me down with his usual 'Let's just take it one day at a time and work with what we can control."

"What do you want him to say?"

"I want him to grieve with me, to ask me what I want, and to cry and scream about how fucking shit the whole situation is. I don't think that's too hard."

"What if it is too hard for him? Maybe that is all he's capable of."

"Maybe, but then he needs to get in the fix-up room. I can't get away from this, there's no get-out-of-jail-for-free card for me. You'd think when someone is dying, people would be able to put their own egos aside."

"To do what you want them to do?"

Whack. Silenced again.

"Yes. My life, my rules."

I should have said 'death' and owned it. Man.

Tick, tick, tick.

"And you know what really sticks in my craw? I've done everything right, all the things you're supposed to do: GCSEs, A-Levels, university. Travel. Career. But it hasn't made a fucking difference. I'm still gonna die a massively premature death."

Tick, tick, tick. I think he revels in the silence. In my discomfort.

"But other times I think it doesn't really matter. Who cares? Shit happens and sometimes shit happens to you. We can't take it for granted that we'll automatically get eighty years and plan accordingly."

"*You* can't take it for granted, you mean."

"No, I guess not," I said, flaccid and spent.

Tick. Tick. Tick.

I see him checking the clock. "Our time has nearly come to an end and I just want to take a few minutes to reflect on our process."

Process?

"Can you give me two reasons why this session worked for you?" I didn't expect a test or to be asked to applaud his skill. My mind becomes a cavernous black hole. Nothing. The wind howls as tumbleweed rolls across the floor.

"I guess you've challenged me and I like being challenged, especially about my language. And I feel safe." This is a lie; I don't feel safe. He was too familiar, too invasive, far too soon. Ignoring the doubts worming their way up from my unconscious, I let my need to be the good student overwhelm my gut. Compliance is more comfortable than failure. I don't do failure.

But I'm failing at life.

As soon as the lift doors close, my brother Ed says, "You know who he reminds me of?" He's eager for me to play his game, but can't contain himself. "Lovely Stu. You know, from *Peep Show*."

"I don't remember."

"You must. The beautiful, kind monk that Jez falls in love with."

I think for a moment, processing all the episodes of *Peep Show* I've ever seen, until I find Lovely Stu. "Oh yes, I do remember now. It's perfect—he is Lovely Stu!"

"Watch out. Nobody's that nice."

"You're too cynical."

"And you're too trusting. Did you talk about me?"

"It's only the first week—give me a chance."

The weather improves by just a few degrees and he abandons his socks. His naked ankles are extraordinarily disconcerting. Smooth, tanned skin running over perfectly curvaceous anklebones. I feel like a Victorian gentleman near on bursting with arousal at the glimpse of a woman's naked wrist. I'm also crying, torn between my grief and his glow. He stops me mid-wail.

"That's all very well, but I just get the sense you're not here, you're not in the room." My tears continue flowing: I'm grieving at the loss I am going to inflict on my sister and her two small children. He presses on, wanting me to himself. "What do you feel now, in this moment?"

Like a twat. I feel like a twat.

"I don't know what you mean."

Aren't my tears enough?

"I feel like you save up topics to talk about."

"I do—isn't that how this works? There's stuff that upsets me during the week and I want to talk about it."

"But what do you feel now, in the room, between us?"

I wasn't aware there was an 'us'.

"I feel relieved about dealing with something I've

needed to talk about all week but couldn't because there was no one who would listen until I got here, with you."

"You always do that?"

"Isn't that what everyone does to fulfil the tedium of the social contract?"

"No wonder you're now lonely. You're used to managing your relationships and now you can't because your disease isn't interesting to others, it's frightening. I think you have issues with spontaneity."

Wanker. How's that for spontaneity?

"What did you talk about today?" Ed doesn't even wait for the lift to arrive.

"My apparent lack of spontaneity."

"Boring. Is that all?" Ed is testy.

"According to Jude, I can't talk about my trauma at inflicting death on our nieces."

"Yeah, yeah, you're gonna die. Blah blah blah. I think you're too spontaneous."

"I won't tell you anything if you're gonna be like that."

Death, like any new experience, takes time and practice to master. The palliative care specialists have been especially trained to help you die. Dying is their bread and butter. They are an assortment of individuals possessing differing levels of skills: the good, the bad and the totally inappropriate. Nonetheless, the worst of their breed have certain things in common. A standardized head tilt accompanies 'the voice'—a well-practiced sympathetic tone, adopted to work through a list of procedural questions.

The voice. That fucking voice.

A fundamental tension hangs between the dying and the professional. They know death and its technical stages but I know it intimately. They're fantastically knowledgable about it; if they were competing on *Mastermind* it would be their specialist subject. But I'm living it. The Grim Reaper doesn't loiter by *their* side, tapping his skeletal finger against an hourglass fast running out of sand. And they know that too.

When I get to know a palliative care professional, I ask why they've chosen their living amongst the dying. The answers often given are "It's a privilege to share someone's death" or "I meet so many fascinating people."

Jude adds, "True integrity emerges, integrity one wouldn't encounter in any other situation. Dying burns off the detritus of the mundane, the day to day, leaving one's essence a burnished glow of pure energy." He's quietly excited, eyes closed and hands together almost in a prayer.

"No offence, but I'd rather not have any integrity and still have a life."

"Yeah, sure," he says.

He obviously prefers the dying; I'd rather be an arsehole.

Most surveys, which measure job satisfaction, find that hairdressers and beauticians are happiest in their work. Nowhere mentioned are the technicians of death.

"What do you think about me?"

He's broken the fourth wall. Lovely Stu flashes through my mind. I'm not telling him about that—and definitely not about his golden glow of health and sexuality.

"I can't answer that! You're the therapist, the professional that guides the process. It's not about our personal opinions of each other."

"But it's very much about our relationship." No other health professional has ever barged into this forbidden territory. "Be spontaneous. What's going through your mind now?"

"Inappropriate. See? I can be spontaneous."

He pulls half of his mouth into a noncommittal smile.

"Why inappropriate?"

"Because you're paid to do this and this is a professional relationship with certain accepted boundaries. I wouldn't tell my teacher or a boss what I thought of them personally. I also don't think it's relevant."

"You want to know what I think of you?"

"No! Absolutely not. No, no, no."

I do. I'm desperate to know, but I can't endure the humiliation of admitting curiosity.

"Do you care about me as a human being?"

We've only known each other for a total of five hours and he demands a declaration.

"When I heard about the Westminster Bridge attack I did wonder if you were in the area and if you were okay. So yes, I guess on a human level I do care about you."

In the same way I care for any other human being.

"Okay, that's a good start. Anything else?' Staring down at his naked ankles, his beautiful ankles, I claw together a vanilla response.

"I think you're at ease with yourself and I imagine you can deal with most things that arise in life fairly easily.

You're good to your wife and don't kick children on the way to work."

"I'm not afraid of dying," he adds.

Insult to injury comes to mind.

"I don't believe you. You can't truly know how you're going to feel until you're actually facing it."

"I just know. There are some things that you just know." I think he misunderstands the finality of death. There is no novelty T-shirt that reads "My mum went to the other side and all I got is this lousy T-shirt".

"But you can't test that, you can't possibly anticipate your feelings."

"Okay. You say you think I'm good to my wife and I don't kick children on the way to work. How do you know?" He forges on, not allowing me to answer. "You can't test it, you just know it's true."

A secret camera and a private detective would do the trick.

"I think there's something I'm missing with Jude."

"It's all this hippy-dippy nonsense. I wouldn't trust a man who doesn't wear any socks."

"He asked me what I think of him personally. Do you think it's a bit weird and creepy?"

"Talking to a stranger is all a bit weird and creepy. Has he asked you about sex yet? I bet he will. It's what they do, pry into people's sex lives. Perverts."

"Is it the type of therapy? Is it him? I've never been dying before, so it could be that. But something isn't right."

"I could have told you that."

"It's a kind of sexual relief," I admit, laughing. "My genitals are on fire most of the time and I'm forever begging Tom to scratch my vagina, which he complains about no end—he claims scratching someone else is an act of violence—but no matter how much scratching I get, it's never enough. I'd crawl over broken glass for more scratching. It's like being a heroin addict. I'm pretty sure I didn't get this itchy before I was sick."

"I'm sure you did, but because you can't scratch yourself, you're more aware of it."

Arrogant bastard.

"I'm paraphrasing, but the man who can scratch his own itch is a free one, says Callicles, the Greek philosopher."

"Great metaphor," I concede.

"Are you able to get much sexual pleasure?"

Ed was right, dammit.

But I'd been waiting for his sex talk and was prepared. I'd face off his golden glow. "It's pretty tough when you can't move. Bearing any weight and stretching my legs is painful. Pleasure is kind of fleeting."

"Sexuality is a crucial part of human existence. Broadly speaking, there are three things people are usually most concerned with: sleeping, eating and fucking." He can't shock me with swearing: my dad's favourite phrase is "you stupid motherfucking, cunting fuck-pig".

"Wearing a ventilator mask, looking more like a World War II fighter pilot and sounding like Darth Vader is less than alluring. But then I guess it could be some kind of kinky sex game."

"The logistics, as you say, may be problematic, but you still have sexuality."

"I dream about sex all the time. Almost no one is safe and, in my dreams, anything goes. That's where I get my relief. In reality, sex has become just another thing to work at."

"Is it worth making the effort, though, no matter how hard it is? It's tough to close down on a whole aspect of your humanity."

"I received an interesting offer from an excolleague. He sent me a message asking if I needed someone to make me cum. He also added that he couldn't imagine me being able to ask or anyone offering. So I guess he thought he would. I laughed aloud when I read it. It was generous and inappropriate. I'm continually shocked about how people react to my illness and at least he was facing it head on, so to speak."

"Is it something you'd want to try?" He physically oozed, seeping into my personal space. As his legs sprawled across the floor, his naked toes rested centimetres from my own. I couldn't withdraw my feet.

Manspreading has an entirely new dimension when stuck in a wheelchair.

"I don't think Tom would approve."

It was obvious he was enjoying himself. The unspoken offer stood between us. His golden glow versus my leaden misery was hardly a balanced match, and a weaker individual might have submitted.

"I bet you were tempted—how could you resist Lovely Stu?"

"What the fuck! Anyway, I couldn't be certain."

"So if you were certain, you'd do it?"

"No! Of course not, for Christ sake. I didn't mean it like that."

Ed nodded to my reflection in the lift mirror, flicked the bobble on my woolly hat and said, "You should go for it. It's not like you're gonna get any offers from anywhere else."

He was slumped down in his chair with his eyes half closed, as if snoozing in the garden on a sunny afternoon. "Are you sleeping?" My tone was sharp.

"No. I'm listening, absorbing. I'm in a slow mode, able to sit with what's going on and wait. You're in a fast mode, you want to get everything over with."

He could sit with what's going on but I wanted him to look like he gave a shit and open his eyes.

"You look like you're not listening."

"Are you used to not being listened to?"

OMG! Listening's supposed to be his job. Looking like Sleeping Beauty ready to be awakened by true love's kiss isn't exactly helping with my issues of isolation and loneliness.

"Do you mind opening your eyes?"

"Okay, if it's challenging for you."

No, it's just good manners.

"Is it challenging for you to be told off?"

"I didn't realise I was being told off."

"You were." I tried to soften my anger and added, "A bit." His 'let's just see how far I can push you to tolerate your boundaries being crossed' attitude was a pain in the arse and I'd lost again.

"It's like he's playing a game and I can't work out the rules."

"You've always been a bit naïve: a mouse for anyone to toy with." Ed dipped my chair backwards. "Hands in the air—we're on the rollercoaster!"

He dropped the chair down again until the back of my head touched the floor. Screaming, I shouted, "Sto-o-o-p! Ed pleeaase!' He was laughing so hard, that he couldn't speak. "You fucking little twat. That was fucking dangerous."

As he wiped the tears of laughter from his eyes, he replied, "Some people just can't take a joke."

"I've been to my palliative care consultant to discuss how much longer I've got." He leans forward, eager. "She told me that if I eat well and avoid infections, I should live quite a while."

He physically wilts. Our roles are changing; I know what he is now.

Recovering from the blow at learning I might live more than a few months, he continues. "What do you still want from this therapy?"

I remember my lie—that I felt safe. I feel lonelier than when I started. Now I know what is wrong between us and I make my attack. "I want to talk about the difficulty in our relationship." He nods with his trademark tiny moves. "I get the feeling this process is about you and in some way your personal development." He's unshaken, as expected.

"That's perceptive of you. Very. Most people wouldn't

operate on that level of understanding. Jaspers states that we should all live at the boundary of what's comfortable and then push that boundary back, always living at the edge of our comfort zone."

I knew it! I fucking well knew it!

He wants to live at the edge of his comfort zone. A place I already inhabit whether I want to or not. These sessions haven't been about me getting it wrong because I don't understand the process of dying or his style of therapy. It's about him. It always has been. He must have thought it was all his Christmases come at once when I was wheeled through the door.

"A bit like psychological extreme sports," I suggest.

"I wouldn't have put it quite like that, but yes." He is a psychological vampire sucking in his patients' tragedy, building his resilience, nourishing himself on misery. Thanks to me, his interior world grows, becoming richer, more nuanced, more exquisite. As I become weaker, he becomes stronger.

"Well, I don't particularly want to be another notch on your death post. I wouldn't be surprised if you keep a bloody spread sheet of everyone who has died, with a section noting special features so you'd remember who they were."

He withdraws his beautiful ankles and crosses his feet beneath his chair. "I do undertake this job with compassion for my clients and the relationships are not straightforward. When we interact the power balance shifts back and forth between us. Sartre put it well when he said that relationships resemble a handshake. Sometimes I'll be shaking your hand, sometimes you'll be shaking mine and sometimes we'll be shaking hands together."

"And you have a firm grip."

"I'm sorry you feel that way, but I can assure you there is no death post."

There definitely is.

He continues. "I'm glad you've been able to tell me how you feel and we've had this chance to clear the air. How do you feel?"

Smug. Like Colombo, hoisting the guilty by their own petard.

"More equal, I guess. We are shaking hands now, instead of me feeling your icy grip." I force a laugh.

Not-so-lovely Stu now.

"Now we can go forward and start again on a more equal footing, and I'll make sure I warm my hands before each session. Shall we book in the next appointment?"

"So what did you talk about this week? Anything juicy?"

"The therapist/patient relationship mainly."

"How tedious can you get? When's your next appointment?"

"Two weeks."

"When the hell are you going to get round to talking about me?"

...

I've been told you have cancelled our session and don't want to rearrange. I urge you to come back and at the very least have one last session to debrief and

summarise. I think it is of importance to you. Please
call me back.

I don't think so. You may need to debrief, mate, but I
don't. And I may be a raspberry ripple but at least I'm
not chicken jalfrezi.

I've escaped from his golden glow and I'd rather chew
my own useless legs off than let that psychopath feed on
my death again. He has helped me to understand. To
understand I'm radically alone and death is the most
personal experience of our lives; no therapist, expert,
friend or lover can make sense of it for us.

My death is mine alone, and I will own it.

ACKNOWLEDGEMENTS

For most, lockdown has been a depressing and unpredictable time. Our everyday lives have mutated without hope of returning to pre-COVID reality. Change has been demanded of us and we must learn to coexist with our wily COVID companion, whilst ensuring that not only the most vulnerable in society are protected but that Key Workers are also fully supported and respected.

There is, for some of us, an advantage. Society has moved online, which means I no longer have to check wheelchair accessibility, arrange a chaperone and prepare my partner to go through the arduous task of readying me for the outside world (spare ventilator battery: check, painkiller: check, blankets: check). It's tedious at best. Now, I am free to join whatever event I fancy! The world has come to me—courses (Spread the Word Writing Retreat, Starting Your Novel at City Lit), concerts (Kylie, Jarv Is) and events (Q & A with Kazuo Ishiguro, live tellings of M.R. James stories), some that would previously have been impossible for me to attend – the rooms above pubs don't tend to be wheelchair friendly: "We can try to carry you up the narrow steep set of stairs?" … "No, thanks—I'm okay for a primitive and terrifying fairground experience." Without online festivals, my books wouldn't have been found by Carla Girard at Mercuria Press, and finally without Alodie Fielding's beautiful illustrations, it is unlikely that Carla would have noticed them in the first place.

I feel as if I have come home to a place where like-minded creatives share a love of books as beautiful objects, sensual experiences encompassing the physical, visual and imaginative. Dark tales told with a light touch. We are a perfect fit. So thank you, Carla—I anticipate many literary adventures together. Thank you also for your appreciation of the fruitful relationship that Alodie and I share. Thank you, Alodie—let's keep the creativity coming…

Thanks to Katie Isbester at Claret Press, who initially took a risk by publishing my story collections and for which I am ceaselessly grateful. Katie has also been true to her ambition of elevating my work to the next level in the 'food chain.' Thanks, Katie. Huge thanks to Madi Simcock-Brown also at Claret Press for her endurance when figuring out the Frankfurt Book Festival website. Love and thanks to Laura Emsden, not only for her superb and quick grasp of my texts, but her forensic proof-reading skills. Laura, I love you for your insight, advice and our continuing friendship. Thanks to Ginny Wood for the original book design and for bringing flair to all of our projects, whether books, pamphlets or branded merchandise. Ginny, it is always a pleasure to work with you.

During lockdown my partner—Jonathon Cartwright-Tickle—and I were shielding in our 'lofty tower' (top floor flat), we took care of each together in our team of two and he has my enduring love and gratitude. Thank you,

Jonathon, without you I would be able to achieve very little.

For your exemplary care, despite the difficulties of lockdown, I especially thank Dr. Michelle Ramsay and Shauna Sheridan at the Lane Fox Respiratory Unit, St Thomas's Hospital, and Dr. Cathy Ellis and Dr. Rachel Burman from the Motor Neurone Disease Clinic at King's College Hospital. Enormous thanks to everyone at the Guy's and St Thomas's Community Palliative Care Team, and Jonathan Bose, Jacqueline Edmead and Iain Stringer (formerly) of the Southwark Neuro Conditions Team, Guy's and St Thomas's NHS Foundation Trust.

Additional thanks to my family and also to my 'Short Story Supper Club' partner-in-rhyme Josephine Rydberg, to Sandrine Ceurstemont for making my website look fabulous, and Rachel Wegh and Diana Mukuma for their support and friendship.

This is a new adventure, so thank you all for coming with me this far in the journey. Onwards…

Sarah Gray
October 2021

S arah Gray has been story-telling all of her professional life. As a writer and filmmaker she is delighted by what she fears and loves to explore the darkly comic side of the human psyche. In a scary and illogical world there is plenty to allow her imagination free reign.

Stories enable us to face the worst that can happen and then get back to everyday life, pretending the terrible stuff only happens to other people. In October 2015, Sarah's fears were realized when she was diagnosed with Motor Neuron Disease. Since then she has been learning how to adapt to chronic disability and adjusting to the horror of a terminal illness.

Visit Sarah's website at sarahgrayracontesse.com.

A lodie Fielding is an artist and illustrator who lives and works in London. She originally trained as a painter and printmaker and completed an MA in illustration in 2008. She has since gone on to illustrate books for several authors, as well as provide illustrations for magazines, CD cover art and other varied projects including mural painting.

Her work is influenced by fairy tales, myths and urban legends but she also draws inspiration from popular culture, including fairground, circus and theatre artwork. It is however, the themes found in folklore that she returns to time after time. "My work sometimes strays from these themes, but I usually find myself drawn back to the forest."

Visit Alodie's website at thecrookedstyle.com.